Best Wishes,
K.M. Swan

Acknowledgments

To my husband, who made all of this possible, and to the readers of *The Loft*, *Catherine's Choice*, *Sarah* and *The Journals*, who encouraged me to continue writing.

Cover design by

Michael A. Swanson

Regrets

by

K.M. SWAN

ISBN 0-9677749-4-2

~Introduction~

She was standing at the kitchen sink when the doorbell rang. It no longer startled her, as it had been nearly five years. She dried off her hands and went to the front door. Smiling, she opened the door, and then felt goose bumps rise on her arms when she saw who it was.

"Good morning, officers. What can I do for you?" she said pleasantly.

"Are you Marian Tulley, Ma'am? We'd like to ask you a few questions." With that her shoulders drooped slightly and her smile faded. She wondered how they had found her. It had been almost five years since she left her home, gotten on the bus to come here and began a new life.

"I think you've made a mistake. My name is Laura Holt," she said, with as much confidence as she could muster.

"May we come in, Ma'am? We need to talk to you, and we won't take much of your time," he said it politely, but she knew he wasn't taking no for an answer. She unlocked the outer door and stood to the side so they could enter her home.

"I've just made coffee. Would you like some?" she asked, thinking her voice shook a bit.

"That would be nice," the men said together and sat down at the kitchen table. One of the officers took a pad and pen out of his shirt pocket; she knew it was over now. Then the phone began to ring . . .

~1~

Five Years Earlier

Dr. Robert Tulley was looking over the latest medical journals at his desk in the family room of his palatial home. He had the afternoon off and was taking advantage of the time to catch up on his reading. He and his wife were planning a simple supper at home this evening. He was about to ask her if it was too early for a martini, when he was dealt a blow to the back of his head that took his breath away. Stunned, he tried to turn and look behind him, but was hit again and again and again. He lost consciousness and fell from the chair, tipping it over as he went down. He died right where he landed, without ever knowing what had hit him.

When he failed to show up at the hospital for an early surgery, his colleague took over for him and performed the operation. But when he didn't make rounds on his patients and hadn't arrived at his office by ten o'clock that morning, the phones began to ring.

"Dr. Tulley's office. How may I help you?" the

receptionist said pleasantly when the call came in.

"Dr. Horton here. Is Dr. Tulley in? I'm calling from the hospital - no one's seen him this morning," he told her.

"No, Dr. Horton, he isn't here either. We've called his home several times, but no one answers."

"Not like him to be late for work," Dr. Horton mumbled. "Well, thank you. I'll look into it. Call me here if he contacts you."

"Yes, I certainly will. Would you let us know here if you find out anything? The patients will be coming in soon. I don't know what we'll tell them," she said.

"Yes, of course. I'll do that," he said, replacing the receiver on the phone. He rubbed his chin, removed his scrub cap and scratched his head. This was not like Robert at all. Dr. Horton was concerned now. He picked up the phone and dialed the police department.

He told them who he was and explained the situation. He asked them if they could go to the house and have a look around. They said they'd be happy to, and would get back to him as soon as they could.

Two police officers took the call. They both knew of the doctor, as he was a prominent surgeon in town. They had no trouble finding the house in this prestigious neighborhood, where the homes were beautiful and the cars on the driveways were expensive.

Detective Dawson drove the car up the driveway and parked close to the garage. Nothing looked amiss so far. They got out of the car and walked up to the front door. A neighbor on his porch next door was craning his neck to see what that cop car was doing there. They waved to him and rang the doorbell, waited a bit and rang it again. When, after several minutes, no one came; they walked around to the back of the house. The blinds were closed on the back door so they couldn't see in, but when the detective tried the door, he found that it was unlocked. They entered the laundry room, where everything was in order. They called out to the doctor and his wife, but no one answered. Sgt. Crane pushed the lavatory door open with his foot; nothing there. They opened the door to the garage and saw both cars were there; a Mercedes Benz for each.

"I want a car like that someday," Sgt. Crane muttered.

"Yeah, right. In your dreams," Dawson answered, as he reached inside his jacket and took out his weapon. They made their way into the kitchen, calling out the doctor's name as they went. The table in the eating area was set for two. A candle in the center had burned down to nothing, leaving small drops of wax on the cloth.

It was eerily quiet and both men had an ominous feeling. It looked like the doctor and his wife hadn't eaten dinner the night before. A beef roast was on a cutting board on the counter and a green salad, now wilted, sat waiting to be tossed. Next to that were poor boy buns, sliced, ready for the beef, and two small ramekin dishes held au jus for dipping.

"Looks like they didn't have supper last night," Crane said, as he picked up a bun and tapped it on the counter. "Hard as a rock. Wonder what interrupted them?" he murmured.

"Something big and heavy," Dawson called from the family room.

Crane went into the family room to see for himself.

"Oh, Jesus," he said, staring down at the body. "Any sign of the wife?"

"Not yet, but this guy's been dead for more than twelve hours, I know."

They knew from experience that rigor mortis started at the head and worked its way down, and this body was stiff from head to toe. Livor mortis, the black and blue discoloration of the body due to gravitational pooling of blood, showed that he had been lying there a very long time. The back of the doctor's head was caved in and bloody. Blood, congealed now, trickled from his ears, nose and the corner of his mouth.

"God, did they have to hit him that hard?" Crane asked, bending down to get a closer look. They could almost feel the emotion of the killer as they examined the wounds.

"Looks like someone was very mad at the good Doc," Dawson mumbled.

They carefully searched the rest of the house expecting to find another body, but didn't. Mrs. Tulley was gone. They did find her handbag with credit cards, driver's license and some cash; and, her closet was full of clothes as were the dresser drawers. It didn't look good.

Dawson called headquarters and reported his findings; the coroner would soon come to the house. The Tulley house was cordoned off with yellow police tape, as it was now a crime scene, and subject to a complete forensic investigation.

A search for Mrs. Tulley would be organized and the neighborhood would be combed, as they had found no murder weapon. The neighbors would be questioned as well. Hopefully someone heard something. There was much to be done.

When the coroner arrived, he confirmed that Dr. Tulley had, indeed, been dead for fourteen to sixteen hours. He died from blunt force trauma to the head; more blows than were necessary, indicating great anger on the part of the perpetrator. But who could be angry with this man? His patients loved him and he was revered by the entire medical staff.

The autopsy showed that he had died fairly soon after receiving the blows. His swollen brain pressed on the brain stem, causing his breathing to cease and his heart to stop beating. Mercifully, he had not regained consciousness. His skull was fractured in several places. Who could have done this to such a wonderful man? The entire hospital was grieving.

And what about poor Mrs. Tulley? Had she been abducted? But for what reason? There was much speculation and many rumors floating around the hospital and the neighborhood. A few people whispered that maybe it was a good thing Dr. Tulley was dead, because what would he do without his beautiful wife? It would be so awful for him.

Some wondered if there had been another man involved, but not many believed that. What woman in her right mind would want another man if she had Dr. Tulley? Besides that, her mother was in a nursing home with Alzheimer's disease and had no one but her daughter. No, Mrs. Tulley wouldn't leave like that. The speculating continued.

There was no forced entry, no murder weapon, no finger prints, other than those of the residents and a friend or two. A few fibers were found on the body, but the source had not been found as yet. Not much to go on, and no sign of Mrs. Tulley.

Detective Dawson was obsessed with this case. There was something about it, but he couldn't put his finger on it. He knew as more time passed, the trail would become colder; and there wasn't even much of a trail at this time. There were no unidentified bodies reported in his jurisdiction or the surrounding counties. How could a woman disappear without a trace? He would keep at it long after everyone else gave up. He nearly drove his wife crazy too. She wished he would let it go, and told him so, many times, but he couldn't.

The crime scene unit learned that the fibers found on the body were from an afghan that was draped over the couch in the family room. No surprise there, the man lived in the house, but for some reason Dawson had bagged the blanket and marked it as evidence.

Dr. Tulley's parents wanted to take care of things in the house, but were forced to wait until the investigation was completed. Detective Dawson would often get up early in the morning and go over to the house while it was still a crime scene. He would walk through the place again and again, trying to imagine exactly what had happened that night. He felt sure he was overlooking something obvious, but could not put it together. Somehow it seemed too contrived to him, and still no sign of the woman - she had vanished into thin air. He had the awful feeling that this case would go down in the books as an unsolved homicide, and he hated that.

~2~

Marian and Dr. Tulley met shortly after he joined the staff of Community General Hospital where Marian, much to her parents' disappointment, worked as a nurse's aide. She worked in the pediatric wing, and was on duty when the doctor came to check on a little boy whose appendix he had removed earlier in the day. He caught her eye and she felt herself blush; he was so good looking. When he went to the desk to make a note on the patient's chart, he asked the nurse about the girl he had just seen.

"Why? Are you interested in her?" the nurse asked, rolling her eyes at him. All the nurses flirted with him. He was such a handsome man.

"No, not really. I just thought she looked like someone I know."

"Well, her name is Marian Jacobs and she's the best aide we have. The kids love her and she loves them," she told him.

"That's not who I thought it was then, but she sure does look like her." He cleared his throat and took on a more professional demeanor. "I've left an order for pain medication for Billy if he needs it when he wakes up," he said, handing her the chart.

"Thank you, doctor. I'll take care of that now," she said.

She was ordering the medication when Marian came up to the desk.

"Who *was* that?" Marian asked, her eyes huge with wonder.

"That was Dr. Robert Tulley, and he asked about you!"

"Oh, he didn't! Stop teasing me. Gosh, he's good looking, isn't he?"

"Yes, he is, that's for sure and I'm not teasing you. He asked who you were. He said you looked like someone he knew," she explained.

"Oh, I don't know him, but I'd like to," Marian said, and went back to her work. After that day it seemed as though Dr. Tulley stopped in on the pediatric unit more often than normal. He wanted to get to know this Marian Jacobs.

~~~

Marian Jacobs was an only child. Her parents, Vivian and Earl, were in their forties when she was born. They had never longed for a child and were quite content with their life together as it was. However, when it became apparent that a baby was on the way, they were amused with the idea of having a child. By the time their little girl arrived they had accumulated enough for three babies. They knew very little about children, so they bought everything in sight.

Marian was a fairly easy baby to care for; she nursed well and slept much of the time. As she grew into a small child, her parents learned that if they
~~~

gave her everything she asked for, she was quite pleasant. She was given no direction whatsoever, and seldom, if ever, heard the word *no.* Her parents thought their only obligation was to make sure their little girl was happy at all times, or, at the very least, content. She was a petite child with light brown hair and deep blue eyes. She was pretty and got along well with everyone.

When, at the age of five, she expressed a desire to take tap dancing lessons, she was enrolled in a dance class within the week and owned tap shoes and several costumes. Three weeks later, when she said she would prefer tumbling, she was allowed to do that. Then there were violin lessons, ballet lessons, gymnastics and finally the flute. She tried everything and finished nothing, but she was *allowed* to do it.

She did well in school and gave them no cause for concern, so they assumed they were doing the right thing. High school was a different story, however. She still made good grades, but she much preferred the "after school hours" to her time in school; shopping, parties, movies, and just indulging herself in whatever pleased her.

In the first quarter of her junior year, she announced to her parents that she had no intention of going to college. Her father nearly hit the ceiling.

"Of course, you're going to college, and this, young lady, is a very important year. All testing for further education is done now, and you'd better shop around because you're going to have to apply somewhere soon," he told her.

"I said I don't want to go," she said, looking at

her mother with a puzzled expression. "Why in hell would I do something for four years that I don't want to do?"

"You watch your language, Marian, or I'll take away your car!" her dad exclaimed. Oh, of course she had a car and she didn't so much as pay for the gas to run it. They couldn't understand their daughter. They had given her everything she ever wanted and now she was behaving this way. They simply had no idea that parenting meant guiding, loving and disciplining, not just making sure the child was completely happy at every moment.

Marian's friends envied her freedom and all the material things she had. That was normal; but when she was at a friend's house, she would watch the way they interacted with their parents and it was nothing like her home. She liked the way her friends' mothers told them what time they were expected to be home when she picked them up in her car. It seemed as though their mothers worried about them, or at least were concerned. She always got home at a decent hour, not because she was told to, but when her friends went home, so did she. This gave her own parents the impression that they were parenting.

Most of her friends were looking forward to going to college, but they couldn't convince Marian. She was unfocused and had no direction in life.

After many heated discussions, it was decided that Marian would take one year after high school to plan her future. This was somewhat embarrassing for her parents as all of their friends' children were college graduates. They made excuses for her, saying that because she was such a good girl, they wanted her to take her time and make her own decision.

The year after Marian graduated, she waited tables for a while, then quit that and did nothing. She applied to three colleges later in the year and was accepted by all of them. She chose the one farthest from home and knew that everything would be paid for by her father.

She did well in college, but nothing really interested her. She had no vision as to what her life would be, so after two years, she quit. She was twenty-one years old with no thought about the future. She moved back home with her parents and did whatever she pleased. She had several jobs, but none with any long-term appeal. Two years later when she told her parents that she would like to have her own place, they were in complete compliance.

"Look in the paper after supper," her dad said. "Pick out a few and we'll go look at them." There was no mention of her being able to pay the rent; that would be taken care of for her. In later years, Marian puzzled over the fact that not one of them, she, her mother or her father, thought at the age of twenty-three she should be supporting herself.

A small apartment was found and everything needed to furnish it was purchased for her. All the bills went to her father. Her parents, thinking they had done well for her, were now enjoying the house to themselves again.

~3~

Six months after she moved into the apartment, Marian started working at the local hospital. She was a nurse's aide on the pediatric ward and she loved it. It was the first time she had found something she liked to do, and she considered going into the nursing program there. She only toyed with the idea, however. Not only did she dread the thought of school again, but she would have to give up her job in pediatrics.

She learned a great deal at the hospital and began to realize just how tunneled her vision had been. These little patients were so brave, she couldn't believe it, and so were their parents. It was incredible. She really hadn't had many life experiences. She had always done what she wanted, to do, period.

When a little girl died of leukemia, Marian became more emotional than she had ever been before. She was filled with something she had never known. It was so difficult to watch the parents of that little girl as she lay dying, and it seemed to Marian that they may die too, as their pain was so great. She had never experienced that kind of emotion. She loved her parents and supposed they loved her, but this was something different. She decided then and there that she wanted more from life; but at the same time, she was confused.

She worked hard at her job and the kids loved her; she did extra things for them too. She read to them or they played cards if she had time, and sometimes she sat and rubbed a little one's back. She was consumed with her work. It was all new to her and she loved it.

When she had been working several months and gotten to know some of the employees, she began to realize that she was the only one who wasn't paying her own way. Some of the girls were much younger, still in school, and living with their parents; but she was the only one living off of her parents and away from them. It was an odd situation, but no one criticized her - to her face anyway. One of the older nurses talked to her about it one day, when they were having lunch together.

"I'll bet you would be very proud to be able to care for yourself. You should think about it," she told Marian. "What do you do with your money if you don't pay for anything?" she asked her, then added, "If you don't mind my asking."

"No, I don't mind. I put a lot of it in the bank and just spend some if I want something," Marian told her casually.

"Your parents don't object?" the older nurse wondered.

"No, actually it was their idea," she said. The woman couldn't figure this out at all. She had children of her own and her goal had always been to help them stand on their own feet. This was very odd.

"Well, you should try it. It's very important for a woman to be able to care for herself in this day and age," she said, hoping the girl would take her advice. She liked Marian a lot and wanted to see her succeed on her own.

Marian did think about the talk they had at lunch, and after work, back at home, she looked over all her expenses. She had saved more money than she realized; maybe she could do it herself. Her apartment was small and not very expensive; everything in it was paid for - thanks to her dad. Maybe she would be able to do it. It was starting to sound like a good idea and it made her feel proud somehow. She was learning things now that most people learn as small children from their parents.

When she ran the idea by her dad, he told her what he thought.

"Are you going to be a nurse's aide all your life, Marian? Why don't you let me pay for some more schooling so you can be *something*."

But, wasn't she something? Whatever did he mean? She didn't know. They had raised her to be exactly the way she was and now they weren't satisfied with her behavior, but not one of them understood it. She did however, in time, pay her own way, and her nurse friend had been right. It felt good.

She began dating a boy who worked in the x-ray department. She had never dated very much, maybe because she had everything she needed; a car, money and anything she wanted. She liked him. His name was Trevor and they had fun together. Her parents liked him, but were not impressed. They would have preferred a radiologist to an x-ray technician.

Then she met Dr. Robert Tulley and everything changed.

~4~

Marian was twenty-six years old when she and Robert met, he was thirty-two. He had joined the surgical group at Community General Hospital right after completing his residency. The group consisted of three physicians who were delighted to have him. He was younger than they were, intelligent and very charismatic. They were quite certain he would bring in lots of new patients, and he did indeed. Every patient wanted him to be the one to cut them open. It was said that women would willingly give up their gallbladders just to have him care for them. He was unbelievable. The other doctors in the group called him the Golden Boy, as their patient load increased. The hospital administrators were pleased as well when patients insisted on admission to Community General so they could be treated by the good doctor.

Marian couldn't believe it when he first asked if he could take her to dinner. She felt her face redden while turning away from him to collect her thoughts.

"Yes," she answered, smiling at him. "I think that would be nice, thank you."

He told her what restaurant he had in mind, if it was okay with her. Then he asked if seven o'clock the following Saturday evening would be all right.

"That sounds perfect. I'll be ready," she said, wondering what she would wear as she wrote down her address for him.

He arrived promptly at seven o'clock, carrying a small bunch of flowers for her. He was even more handsome in a suit than he was in scrubs, if that was possible, and the flowers were just the right touch. He handed them to her and she put them to her nose, inhaling their fragrance.

"They're beautiful. Thank you, Robert. Come into the kitchen and I'll put them in some water," she said, as he followed her through the hallway.

"This is a nice place you have here," he said, looking around. "I like it."

"Thanks. It's small, though, but it's big enough for one," she said, filling a vase with water from the tap.

"Are you ready to go?" he asked.

"Yes. I'll just get my coat."

~~~

Dinner was wonderful and he spared no expense. He was wooing her and it was working. She was absolutely entranced with this man. She wondered what she had ever done to deserve this. Afterward they walked around the small lake behind the restaurant. When she shivered and pulled up her collar, he put his arm around her and suggested they go somewhere for coffee.

"That sounds great! It's colder than I thought tonight. I should have worn a warmer coat," she said.
~~~

"Well, you weren't expecting to be outside," he said, opening the car door for her. "It will be summer soon anyway, and then we'll complain that it's too hot," he said laughing. It was springtime. The cold winter was past and he was right, soon it would be hot.

They talked at length over coffee and learned much about one another. He was the son of a doctor, and had always wanted to become one. He discovered that she wasn't sure what she wanted to do, but someday she wanted to be married. Since she had been working with children, she knew that she wanted her own too. Marian was a bit surprised to hear herself say that as she had never given much thought to the future.

"Oh, I'd like to settle down someday too. Maybe soon," he said. "I'm over thirty you know."

"Well, that's not old," she told him, and then ventured asking if he wanted children.

"Me? Oh, yes. I love kids. I'd like several, if possible," he said, smiling at her.

She returned his smile. That was just what she wanted to hear.

When he brought her home, he stepped inside the door and kissed her softly on the lips.

"I had a wonderful time," he whispered. "I'd like to do it again."

"I would too. Thank you for everything," she said, feeling herself quiver all the way down to her toes.

She talked with Trevor the following week. She hated to hurt him, but she wouldn't see him again. He did feel bad, as he liked her a lot, but knew he couldn't compete with the Golden Boy.

Robert and Marian were seeing each other regularly now and she told her parents about him. They were ecstatic, to say the least, and eager to meet him. They wouldn't care now if their daughter cleaned other people's toilets for a living. She was bringing home a *doctor!* They quickly set a date to have the two over for dinner so they could meet this new man in their daughter's life. Robert's parents lived in another state, so it would be awhile until they would both have the time to go and visit them.

The dinner was planned for a Saturday evening. It was two weeks away, but the wheels of planning were in motion. Earl went to the meat market to inquire about the finest cut of beef. He and Vivian wanted to serve prime-rib, but it had to be just the right cut and cooked to perfection. He hurriedly made notes as the butcher told him how to prepare the meat.

He ordered the beef and told the butcher he would pick it up in the morning on the day of the dinner. Then it was on to the liquor store. Red wine was discussed at length with the proprietor of the store. A very expensive French Bordeaux was chosen. It would be served at room temperature, and opened a few minutes before pouring to allow it to *breathe.* Marian had never seen her parents fuss this much for anyone before. It was a bit confusing for her, but she was grateful that they were so eager to meet Robert and to please him.

When the day of the dinner arrived, Earl and Vivian were ready. The house was spotlessly clean.

The silver was polished and the crystal sparkled. Drinks and hors d' oeuvres would be served before dinner. Not sure what the doctor drank or if he drank at all, Earl had several choices on hand to offer. Vivian had labored over the hors d' oeuvres, trying several different ones in the week before the dinner. She narrowed it down to two. She would serve cheese truffles which were cold, and crab puffs which were served warm. The cheese truffles would be prepared early in the day and refrigerated. Never having tasted Brie cheese before, Vivian didn't care for it, but when combined with butter and cream cheese it was really quite good. Then the concoction was formed into small balls, rolled in dark rye bread crumbs and placed in tiny candy papers. The crab puffs could be made up early, but needed to be placed under the broiler until lightly browned and then served immediately. That would be done when their guests arrived. The meat would be out of the oven, resting by then too. They had planned this evening with precision.

~5~

Robert was a bit early picking up Marian on Saturday. He wanted to be alone with her for a little while before meeting her parents.

"I'm a little early," he told her. "I hope you don't mind."

"I don't mind at all. I'm ready, but let's sit down. We have time."

He sat on the couch and patted the empty spot next to him. Marian smiled and went to sit beside him. He put his arm around her.

"I know we haven't known each other very long, Marian, but I want you to know that I really care for you," he said.

She moved closer to him and said, "I feel the same way, Robert." She couldn't believe it! This seemingly perfect man cared for her. She was floating on air, and when he kissed her she felt faint. She wished they didn't have to be at her parents in twenty minutes, but reminded him that they did.

"I suppose we should leave soon. I'm sure my parents are all ready, and they are very eager to meet you. I told them what a nice guy you are."

"Well, thank you for that," he said smiling. "It's always awkward meeting parents, don't you think?"

"I don't think you'll feel that way. My parents are nice," she told him.

"Good. Well, are you ready to go?" he asked.

"Yes. I'll just get my purse." She went into the bedroom, checked herself in the mirror once more and picked up her purse.

"All set," she said, making sure she had her door key. "Just push that button in and the door will lock, Robert." He pushed in the button and closed the door, trying it once to make sure it was locked. Then he took her arm and led her to the car, opening the door for her and closing it softly when she was seated.

He's so polite, Marian thought, as she waited for him to reach the other side of the car. When he got into the car, he reached over the seat and picked up a bunch of flowers wrapped in pretty paper that he had on the back seat.

"These are for your mother," he said, handing them to her.

"Oh, how sweet, Robert! She will love them," she said, thinking what a prize this man really was.

When they drove up in front of her old home, her parents were watching from the window. They saw Robert walk around to Marian's side of the car and open the door for her. He took her hand and helped her out of the car. They saw she was carrying something wrapped in paper and watched her give it to Robert.

"Oh, he's so handsome, Earl!" Vivian whispered.

"Yes, and polite too," Earl said. "Looks like a fine man to me." They hurried away from the window as the couple approached the porch. Marian rang the bell and opened the door. It was customary for her to walk into her parents' home and not wait to be let in.

"We're here," she called, as her parents came from the kitchen.

"Robert, I'd like you to meet my mother and dad. Mom, Dad, this is Robert," she said beaming.

"Very nice to meet you, Doctor," Earl said, pumping Robert's hand.

"Yes, Doctor. It's wonderful meeting you," Vivian said, reaching for his hand and curtsying just the slightest.

"I'm pleased to meet you, Mr. and Mrs. Jacobs," Robert said. "But please call me Robert."

"Only if you call us Earl and Vivian," Earl said, with a broad grin.

"All right, it's a deal, Earl," Robert said, handing the flowers to Vivian.

"These are for you," he said, flashing his perfect smile for her.

"Oh, they're beautiful! How very thoughtful of you," she said, feeling her knees quiver a bit.

"Something smells wonderful, Mom. What are you making?"

"You'll see, but first we'll have a drink and some appetizers. How does that sound? Now if you'll excuse me for a moment, I have something in the oven, and I want to put these in water," Vivian said, going to the kitchen.

The crab puffs were browned to perfection. Everything was ready. Vivian was grinning, as she arranged the crab puffs on a plate. "A doctor!" she whispered to herself. She placed the flowers in one of her best vases and put it on the buffet in the dining room.

"So, name your poison, Doctor. I mean Robert. What would you like to drink?" Earl asked.

"Well, what do you have?" Robert asked, not wanting to embarrass him by asking for something he didn't have.

"Almost anything you can think of - just name it," Earl said proudly.

"How about scotch, do you have that?"

"The best!" Earl said. "How do you like it?"

"On the rocks, please," Robert said.

Marian was a bit surprised. She had never known her parents to have a supply of liquor on hand.

When everyone had something to drink, they were seated in the living room. The appetizers were on the coffee table within reach.

"So, Robert, Marian tells us that you're a surgeon," Earl said, starting the conversation.

"Yes, sir. I am. I've wanted to be one since I was a little kid. My dad's a doctor, so I was exposed to a lot of medical things as a boy. I guess it was meant to be," Robert said.

Vivian could hardly keep her eyes off of him. If she had been a religious woman, she would have been praying right over the appetizers that these two would marry.

"Mom, these are so good. I don't remember you making them before," Marian said, as she popped a cheese truffle into her mouth. The only appetizer

Marian could remember was squirt cheese on a Ritz cracker.

"I don't believe I've made them before. It's a new recipe," Vivian told her.

"I'm going to check on the roast," Earl said, excusing himself. "It should be ready to slice now. Maybe I should let you do the cutting, Robert, you being a surgeon and all. Just kidding," he said over his shoulder as he went out to the kitchen, laughing.

The meal was delicious and the wine, superb. Robert knew a bit about wine, and this was a fine choice. They lingered at the table awhile and then the plates were cleared.

"I hope you've saved some room for dessert," Earl said, as he removed the glasses from the table. "Your mother has made creme de menthe parfaits for us."

Vivian was putting the tall glasses on a tray to bring to the table.

"Coffee will be done in a minute," she said, placing a dessert in front of each person. Marian was a little surprised at this too, but didn't say anything. Her parents surely must have knocked themselves out for this dinner. Robert, accustomed to the finer things in life, thought everything was very nice, but not unusual.

They talked over coffee and learned more about this Golden Boy. They approved of him, highly. Now if their daughter could just pull this off, their worries about her would be over.

When Marian thought it was the proper time to leave, she suggested it to Robert. She offered to help wash the dishes, and was turned down. Robert thanked them profusely for the wonderful time and the delicious meal. Vivian and Earl expressed their pleasure that they had come for dinner, and thanked Robert once again for the flowers. Marian's parents considered the evening a huge success.

~6~

After six months and a whirlwind courtship, Robert asked Marian to marry him. She was a little surprised as she hadn't known him very long, but in her heart she knew she would say "yes." They had managed a short trip to visit his parents and that had gone well. She liked them and they seemed to approve of her, even though she wasn't from the same social strata as they were.

It was decided that they would have a small private wedding ceremony where the couple lived, and a gala reception one week later where Robert's parents lived. Marian's parents and the newlywed couple would fly together and stay at the home of his parents for three days. From there the new couple would go on to spend their honeymoon in Hawaii, and Vivian and Earl would fly home.

Robert's parents pretty much took charge of the plans, and Marian thought it odd that they made no excuses for not attending the wedding. They would have an extravaganza at the country club where they belonged. That way they could have "their own people" attend, Robert's mother had told him privately. They even offered to pay for the plane fare for Marian's parents, but Earl thanked them graciously and said that it was not necessary. They did, however, accept their offer to stay in the Tulleys' home. Robert said the house was huge and that it would not be a problem.

It was huge indeed. Marian understood now why Robert, unlike most of his friends who were new doctors, had no loans to repay. His medical school expenses were paid in full by his father. All that was expected of him was that he do well, which he had done.

The wedding was a small affair, but nicely done. Earl and Vivian wanted to show off their new son-in-law to everyone, but kept the guest list small. They went all out, however, on the dinner following the wedding. They were able to have the meal at the country club where Robert belonged. It was a beautiful evening and the food was delicious. The newlyweds spent the weekend at a posh resort; and then it was back to work for them both until the reception in Robert's hometown and the honeymoon.

They stayed at his place now, as Marian's was too small, but they would look for a house of their own as soon as they got back from Hawaii. Robert had already talked with a realtor and described the house and location he wanted, so they would have several houses to look at when they returned.

~~~

The reception was overwhelming to Marian and her parents. They had never seen anything like it before. They couldn't imagine *knowing* so many people, much less inviting them all. Earl thought it
~~~

must have cost Robert's father a small fortune, and Vivian was envious, to say the least.

~~~

The week in Hawaii was wonderful and Marian still couldn't believe her good fortune in finding this man. She had never been happier in her life. They stayed in Honolulu, on the island of Oahu. Their hotel was on Waikiki Beach, and they could see Diamond Head from their balcony. It was breathtaking! They dined on local cuisine in open-air restaurants, shopped endlessly and took long walks on the beach. It was a perfect honeymoon. Robert had planned well and Marian told him often.

They looked at three houses when they returned from Hawaii and agreed on one. It was beautiful and in the best area of the three. It was where Robert wanted to live, in a prestigious neighborhood and not far from the country club where he belonged. It was spacious, bright and Marian loved it, but wondered what they would do with all the rooms. She hinted that they could fill the bedrooms with little Tulleys.

"Of course we will, but not for a while. We have plenty of time," he told her. She agreed with this because she knew she would be busy getting the house settled and she had her job too. But not long after they had moved in and everything was in place, Robert made a statement that surprised her.

"You'll have to quit working now, Marian," he said, one evening over dinner.

"Why would you want me to do that?" she asked stunned. She loved her job, and it was wonderful to come home after working all day to this beauti-
~~~

ful house and be with him. She didn't understand.

"You're a Tulley now, Marian, and Tulley women don't work. You have a checkbook, credit cards, and you can have whatever you want. You don't need to work," he said, and gave her a look as though the subject was closed.

"I know we don't need the money, Robert, but I *need* to work. I love the kids, and I really think I make a difference. I don't want to quit," she said.

"I'm sorry, Marian, but how would it look? My wife, a nurses aide. Really!"

She didn't know what to say, so she stood and began clearing the table.

Did he have the right to tell her what she could and couldn't do? She was at the kitchen sink, when he came up behind her and put his arms around her.

"Please cooperate with me on this, Marian. There are plenty of things for you to do. There's the club and so many of my friends' wives are there. You can sit around the pool all day if you like, or go shopping with them. Have lunch . . . just all sorts of things to do," he told her. But for the first time in her life she found something she liked to do. Did she have to give it up because he said so? She turned to face him and put her arms around him.

"I know what would keep me very busy," she said, smiling at him.

"What's that?" he asked.

"A baby. Our own baby. Wouldn't that be great, Robert?"

"Now we talked about that, remember? And we decided to wait, didn't we?"

"Well, yes, until we were settled in our house,

you said. The house is done, right?"

"We'll think about it some more," he said, and again the subject seemed closed.

Marian wasn't sure what to do, so she didn't argue. When she went to work the next day and gave her two weeks notice, her co-workers said how sorry they were that she would be leaving. She was shocked and embarrassed. She mumbled something about being newly-married and how much there was to do at home. What was wrong with him anyway? Why would he do this to her? She was so angry that she had trouble concentrating on her work; and when she got home, she tried to talk about it some more.

"Marian, I told you. You're a Tulley now. Act like one!" She had fourteen days left of the job she loved.

~7~

Other things were changing too. Robert wasn't home much at all, and when he was, he showed Marian little or no affection. She spent her days at the club with the doctors' wives. They were envious of her and asked often what it was like being married to the Golden Boy.

"Oh, you don't really want to know," she would say laughing.

"Oh, but we do. We do!" they would say. Marian felt close to a few of the women, but not close enough to reveal any of her private life to them. She wished she could. She needed someone to talk to. Her mother was certainly not an option. She thought Robert could walk on water. She was becoming frustrated, but who would understand? He was the perfect husband when they were with other people; but alone, it was a different story. Every woman she knew envied her. How could she say a word? Had she married a man she didn't know?

Two years had passed when Robert announced that they could try to have a child. Marian was elated and grateful that she had been so patient.

They stopped using protection and Marian held her breath each month. And each month Robert would hold her as she cried and told him that she had gotten her period.

"Maybe next month," he would say.

"I hope so," she would sigh.

She chose the room in the house that would be a nursery someday. It was a bright and sunny room with a big closet and room to play. She talked Robert into letting her have it painted and she would stand in the doorway and imagine where she would place the baby furniture.

Thoughts of a baby took a back seat when Marian's mother called to say her dad had a stroke and was in the hospital. Robert was already there when Marian got to her father's room. He was next to her mother with his arm around her. Vivian was crying.

"Mom, what happened?" Marian asked and went to her mother's side.

"He collapsed! Just like that - he went down. I called 911 and they came right away, and Robert was here when we got to the emergency room. I'm so glad," she said, looking up in awe at her son-in-law. Marian walked to the bed and looked down at her dad. He didn't look good at all. She touched his hand and spoke to him, but he didn't respond. He never spoke again, and he died two days later.

Vivian was devastated and didn't know what to do, so Robert took care of everything, including comforting her. He did not, however, comfort his wife. Vivian clung to him during the funeral and all the way to the cemetery. Marian had walked to the new grave behind them, alone and confused. Their friends, who attended the service, marveled at Robert's concern for his mother-in-law, but Marian was left to deal with her emotions alone.

~~~

Six months passed and still no baby. Marian had the odd feeling that Robert wasn't surprised, nor was he disappointed. She was terribly saddened and spoke to her husband about going in for a checkup. He told her it was much too early for that and she should just relax. Wasn't she relaxed? She wasn't allowed to do much else. A woman came two days a week to do the housework and grocery shopping. Marian was learning to cook a bit as Robert thought that was all right for a Tulley woman to do. She tried hard to please him and cook what he liked, but he never seemed interested in her or what she did. Why had he wanted to marry her? She often wondered.

He still fawned over Vivian though and she loved every minute of it.

Marian thought it was nice of him to be so kind to her mother, but she needed him too. She was tired of women telling her how lucky she was to be married to Dr. Robert Tulley. "What I wouldn't give . . . ," they would say to her.

And she would think . . . if you only knew.

Two more years passed. They had been married four years. Marian was not pregnant, and Robert was more distant than ever. Vivian had gone off the deep end after Earl died, even with the help of her illustrious son-in-law. She was hospitalized then, and it was discovered that she had the early symp-
~~~

toms of Alzheimer's disease. Her condition progressed rapidly and she was placed in an exclusive nursing home for patients with the same disorder. It was the best place of its kind in the area, Robert said, and he visited her often. Vivian knew no one anymore, but he continued his regular visits. The nurses there were impressed with his faithfulness and told him so often. Marian visited on occasion, but felt empty. She and her mother were strangers to each other now. Why Robert took the time, she didn't know. Was it because of the compliments he received? She was beginning to think that if Robert Louis Stevenson were alive today, he could have patterned his book, *The Strange Case Of Dr. Jekyll and Mr. Hyde*, after her own husband.

What was happening to him? She was trying so hard, but how long would she have the patience to stay with him? She longed for a child, or at least her old job back, but that was not allowed. She thought she may have to leave. She brought this up in conversation one evening and was shocked at his response.

"You will never leave me, Marian. I will not allow it. Don't even think about it. You belong to me!" he said, raising his voice to her. "And if you try, you will be sorry, believe me," he added.

"Is that a threat, Robert?" she asked.

"No, Marian, it's a promise," he told her.

She slept in the guest room that night and cried for a long time. If she could just have a baby, someone of her very own to love and to love her back. She dreamed of a child that night.

At breakfast the next morning, nothing was mentioned about the previous night. Robert read the headlines on the paper as he ate, and drank his coffee in silence. Marian cleaned up the kitchen and was glad that the cleaning woman wasn't coming today. She could stay home and have the house to herself. She had a book to read; and she wanted to write a note to a friend she had worked with at the hospital, who had recently moved away.

She was rifling through Robert's desk looking for a stamp when she found a statement from a friend of theirs, who was a urologist. Confused, she picked it up and read it. It was for a vasectomy, performed on Robert, almost three years ago. The amount due was circled and the check number with the date was noted. She felt the blood drain from her head and sat down. She opened the bottom drawer of the desk and found the stack of old checks. Having the check number made it easy to find. The canceled check was in Robert's handwriting. It was made out to Dr. William Green and at the bottom he had written, "Thanks, Bill! I owe you one."

Marian felt a rage that she didn't know was in her. All those times he had held her and said, "Maybe next month it will happen" knowing full well that it never would. She was glad to be alone now as she couldn't imagine what she would do if she saw him. Putting everything she had touched back where it was, she went to the bedroom and lay down on the bed. It was then that her plan began to take shape.

~8~

The most difficult part of the planning, for Marian, was keeping her disposition and demeanor the same. It wasn't easy, and she was pushed to the limits. She would still, at times, go to him and tell him that again she wasn't pregnant. He would say the same thing every time; "Maybe next month." It was a game for her now. It fueled her anger and helped give her the energy she needed to take action.

She began putting cash in a drawer of her dresser. That was the easy part as Robert was very generous with money. She had her own account and he added to it each month with no questions asked. She had no idea how easy it was to obtain a false identity. She had a social security card and a California driver's license, safely hidden in her drawer. She had driven into the city, eighty miles from where they lived, to get it. She told Robert that she was going shopping. It wasn't unusual at all for her to do that as she preferred the larger stores there. She bought two dresses, a pants suit and shoes to show him when she came home. A dark sweat suit, one size larger than she wore, and a pair of black sneakers were tucked away in her closet, along with a black baseball cap. She was ready now, just waiting for the opportunity to present itself.

She filled her days with the usual things. Aerobics, massages, manicures, shopping and lunches with the doctors' wives, who belonged to the same club. She saw Sally Green, the urologist's wife, often and wondered what her life was like. Was anyone else going through the same thing? Knowing that no one would believe anything bad about the Golden Boy, she said nothing.

Having no one to talk with, she would lie awake at night next to her sleeping husband and try to think of another plan, but couldn't. He had no intention of changing himself or his life. She was a possession. With her plan well-orchestrated, she was simply biding her time.

The opportunity presented itself quite unexpectedly one Tuesday evening.

"Marian, I'm going to be home tomorrow. I've taken a day to catch up on things. I won't even be on call," he told her.

She felt an odd sensation in the pit of her stomach. Could she go through with it? She reminded herself of the secret vasectomy.

"Well, that will be nice, Robert," she said pleasantly. "What are your plans?"

"Oh, don't worry about me. Do whatever you had planned. I've got a lot of reading to do. I'm sure I'll be busy all day," he said. She wondered if most couples wouldn't be eager to spend the day together and do something special, but she said nothing.

She got very little sleep that night, and left the house around ten the next morning. Robert was still in his robe, reading the paper and having coffee.

"I'll be back later to fix dinner. Would you like French dip tonight? she asked.

"That will be fine. Take your time," he said. It was one of his favorite suppers, and it was part of her plan.

She drove around aimlessly for a long time, thinking about what she would do. "Don't think," she told herself. "If you do, you may lose your nerve."

When she arrived home, Robert was in the family room reading.

"I'm home!" she called to him from the kitchen. He muttered something; and she began setting the table, as though she were getting dinner ready. She opened the freezer and removed the beef that had been there for weeks. Passing through the family room to put her purse in the bedroom, she saw that he was seated at his desk reading. Dropping her purse on the bed, she went into the bathroom and held onto the sink. She was shaking and beads of sweat were forming on her forehead. She splashed her face with water and returned to the kitchen. It was four o'clock in the afternoon. She picked up the frozen beef and went into the family room and walked up behind her husband. She raised the meat over her head.

"Marian, is it too . . ."

All the rage that was bottled up inside of her passed through her arms as she brought her weapon down on the back of his head. He tried to turn, and say something.

"Oh . . . ah . . ." She hit him again and he moaned. She hit him again and again, until he fell from his chair onto the floor. She was shaking so much that she had to lean against the couch.

"Oh, my God!" she whispered, as she looked at his body. Was he dead? She wasn't sure, so she watched for a few minutes. Then she went to him and felt for a pulse in his neck; she couldn't feel it. Picking up the beef, she went to the kitchen, unwrapped it and put it in the microwave to cook it quickly. She poured wine into the glasses on the table and lit the candle in the center, checking the family room often. Nothing had changed there. He was lying exactly where he had fallen from his chair. She couldn't bear the sight of him, and covered his body with the afghan that was on the couch, careful not to let it touch any blood.

Back in the kitchen, she fixed a salad, made au jus and sliced the poor boy buns. Then she went to the bedroom to prepare herself. Everything she would need fit into a dark gym bag and she filled that first. Then she removed her shoes, put them inside and zipped it shut. She had way too much cash to be carrying around, but she would need it. She took off her makeup, applied a moisture cream and nothing else. Then she removed her nail polish and clipped her nails short. She was careful to collect each clipping in a tissue and flush them down the toilet. She could leave no evidence behind.

When she heard the microwave beep, she went to the kitchen and put the beef on a cutting board along with a large knife. She hadn't looked at Robert then, but checked him on her way back to the bedroom. She couldn't see the back of his head very well, but he was bleeding from his mouth, nose and ears. It made her shudder, as she pulled the afghan over him again.

When the sky began to darken, she put the oversized sweat suit on over her clothes and slipped her feet into the dark sneakers. Pulling her hair up into a pony tail, she tucked it all under the baseball cap and put on the tortoiseshell glasses with the plain lenses that were part of her disguise. Picking up the gym bag, she left the bedroom, and passing Robert once again, put the bag on the kitchen table. She surveyed the kitchen and thought it looked exactly as if someone had been interrupted suddenly as they were preparing a meal. It was what she had planned. Once more she went to where her husband lay. She carefully removed the afghan from his body, inspecting it for blood, but saw none, as she had placed it carefully over him, avoiding any. She folded it and hung it on the back of the couch where it had been. It was dark now, so she could leave. Taking one more look at Robert, she picked up the gym bag and left through the back door, leaving it unlocked. As her husband lay stiffening on the floor, Marian left her home, walked into the night, and became Laura Holt.

~9~

Her heart pounded as she walked past her neighbors' homes. At the corner she stopped when a car passed by, bending her head as though she was fumbling for something in her pocket. When it was safe to look up, she saw that it was the neighbor who lived three houses from her.

"I have to be careful," she whispered, quite sure that he hadn't recognized her, but wary nonetheless. She walked the mile or so to the mall and used the pay phone in the parking lot to call a cab. Waiting on the bench at the bus stop, her heart began to slow down, but her head was still spinning. *What had she done?*

When the cab pulled up to the curb, she picked up her bag and let herself into the back seat.

"Where to, Honey?" the cabbie asked, with a cigarette dangling from his mouth.

"Bus station, please," she said in a disguised voice.

"You going on vacation?" he continued.

She wondered why he didn't just drive. "I'm going back home. I've been visiting family here," she told him.

"And where's home?" he asked, lighting another cigarette from the one he had finished. The smoke was getting to her now and she coughed.

"Chicago," she lied.

"You like that city stuff? Too busy for me. Cab drivers there must be nuts!" he said, blowing smoke everywhere. When they passed street lights, the blue haze in the car showed clearly and she felt like gagging. He must have tired of his endless questioning as he was quiet for the rest of the trip. When they arrived at the bus station, she had the money ready and included a nice tip. Not too nice, though, she didn't want him to remember her.

"Thank you," he said, smiling at her. "You come back and see us sometime. Take a break from the big city life."

"I'll do that. Thank you," she said, getting out of the cab. Clutching the gym bag to her side, she went into the bus station and ducked into the restroom. She entered the first empty stall, locked the door and sat down on the toilet with the bag in her lap. She was shaking uncontrollably and put her head down on the bag and started to cry. *What had she done?*

For a few minutes she sat there with her head down and let the tears flow. Then she straightened up, blew her nose and left the stall. Splashing water on her face at the sink, she looked into the mirror, searching for signs of Mrs. Robert Tulley, but saw none.

She left the restroom and stood reading the bus schedule. She chose the bus leaving the soonest and going the farthest. It didn't matter where she went, really, but she wanted to stay in the Midwest area where she was familiar with the weather and the people. She thought she would stand out less that way.

She bought a ticket and sat down on the bench to wait the twenty minutes until departure. Taking a paperback novel from her bag, she pretended to read. She had thought of everything, and didn't want someone sitting next to her with a desire to have a conversation. She was steeling herself to remain composed until she could be alone - whenever that would be. At the designated time, the bus was boarded, the tickets collected and they were on their way. When the bus reached the interstate, the passengers were beginning to settle down a bit. Some spoke in soft voices, while others turned on their overhead lights to read. Marian had a window seat and she stared out at the landscape, leaving her light off. The man next to her made no attempt to speak to her, and she was grateful for that.

If only she could sleep; what a relief that would be, but every time she closed her eyes she saw Robert's body. She stared out the window until her vision blurred, then closed her eyes, willing herself to see anything but Robert. How on earth had she come to this? Was there no other way? She began to reminisce about the good times they'd had and felt her throat tighten. Then she would remember the past few years and become angry all over again. She was tired and very confused. Would she ever be able to pull this off? Could she really become someone else and make a life for herself?

She must have dozed off; because when the bus

pulled into the station and stopped, it startled her. She had decided, during the trip, to take another bus a bit farther. At this station, she changed her clothes in the restroom. Taking off the dark sweat suit and rolling it up tightly, she stuffed it into the bag with the sneakers and cap. She put on her flat shoes that she had in the bag and left the stall. At the sink, she washed her face and hands and combed her hair. She applied moisture cream to her face, a bit of lipstick, and went out to the counter to buy another ticket, looking like a different person now.

The ticket was purchased; this trip would take three hours and was leaving immediately. She thought she would feel safer being just a little farther from her home than she was now. Sitting by the window, waiting for the bus to leave, she saw her reflection in glass as she looked out. This is what she was wearing when she . . . . Oh, God, *what had she done?*

My name is Laura Holt. My name is Laura Holt; she said over and over in her head. Pretending to read her paperback book, she dozed off for awhile, but was awake when the bus pulled into the station. She left in a hurry and went into the station to call a cab. Where would she go?

With a little help from the people inside the bus station, she was able to get a cab and was taken to a motel that was next to a shopping center. This would be very helpful as she had little more than the clothes on her back. She checked into the motel for two nights, thinking she may stay longer, but wasn't sure. She wasn't sure of much of anything just now. She took the key from the desk clerk and asked if there was somewhere close by to eat.

"Our coffee shop is around this corner and down the hall. It's open twenty-four hours a day for our guests, Ma'am," he told her.

With a sandwich in a styrofoam box and a carton of milk in hand, she made her way to the elevator. Her room was on the second floor. She found it and unlocked the door. Inside, she nearly collapsed against the door; then moved to the bed and sat down. Alone at last, the tears came.

"What will I do?" she whispered to no one. "I should have killed myself instead of Robert."

Her stomach growled, reminding her that she hadn't eaten in a long time. She ate the sandwich and drank the milk; then took off her clothes and opened the bed. She curled up in a fetal position and escaped to an abysmal sleep. *What had she done?*

~~~

Back at the Tulley home the investigation continued with little progress. No murder weapon was ever found, and after what seemed like a thousand questions asked, not one of them could be answered. The few leads they had turned up nothing. The feelings of the officers working the case were that Mrs. Tulley had not been abducted, as no call was ever received about ransom for her return, but what could have happened to her?

The funeral for Dr. Tulley was equal to that of a dignitary. All of the main streets in the town were cordoned off for the slow ride to the cemetery. It seemed that the whole town was in attendance. Mrs. Tulley's mother was apprised of what had happened, but was so consumed now with the degeneration of
~~~

her illness that she had no reaction whatsoever and didn't attend the service. It was a difficult day for everyone. Robert's parents were devastated at the loss of their son and confused as to the whereabouts of his wife. They didn't know her very well; but their son had chosen her to be his wife, so they accepted her without question. Had she left him for another man? They couldn't believe that, nor could they believe that someone would have deliberately taken his life. It was just more than they could deal with, and the senior Mrs. Tulley had taken to her bed in the motel after the funeral and stayed there for days. The case grew cold, but would not be forgotten.

~10~

Laura Holt was beginning to come to life. After living in the motel for two weeks, she found a small apartment. Now she had an address and was able to obtain credit cards, open bank accounts, and change her driver's license. Her hair was short and highlighted; and her new driver's license picture looked nothing like the person she had once been.

Her apartment was furnished with the basic necessities only, so far. Her concern now was to find a job; not that she was in need of money at the moment, but it was important that she lead as normal a life as possible. She could not in any way draw attention to herself or to her lifestyle. Every day she searched through the job ads in the morning paper. It was what she was doing this particular morning, when she came across an ad for an assistant care giver in a day-care center. Experience preferred, but not necessary. Will train. She circled the ad, and finished reading the paper. Her plan for today was shopping for some small things for her new home. It really looked bare; but she had done well, finding a place to live and buying a used but decent car all in two weeks time. Still uneasy, she wished she could stay home, but her money would run out in time, she knew.

She shopped for lamps and small accessories for the apartment to make it more like a home, not that she deserved one. Her conscience would not let her rest; she didn't know she had such a good one. With the trunk of her car loaded with purchases, she drove to the day-care center for an interview.

"Laura Holt. It's nice to meet you. Please have a seat," the head woman said to her. "My name is Mrs. Czubachowski, but don't worry. I'm known as Mrs. C around here for obvious reasons. I gave up hope many years ago that anyone could pronounce my name correctly. This is easier for everyone, especially the children."

Mrs. C sat behind the desk and began to ask Laura questions. Surprisingly, she answered them without faltering, and many of the answers were fibs. No, she hadn't worked in many years as she was married and hadn't needed employment. But now she was divorced and on her own. Mrs. C seemed impressed with Laura and told her she would call her within the week, if she was hired or not.

"That way you won't have to sit and wonder. I like to do it that way. Now I'll give you this pamphlet to take home with you. It tells all about our facility here; how we operate, etc. It also includes our employee rules and benefits. You'll know what's expected of us and what we expect of you, if you're approved. Do you have any questions?" Laura didn't, and stood to shake the woman's hand.

"Thank you for your time, Mrs. C. I look forward to hearing from you."

She was happy to escape to the privacy of her car once again. She hadn't talked to any one person that much since . . . leaving home. It was unnerving.

At home, she unloaded the trunk of her car and carried the bags inside. Her apartment was like a small house: one bedroom, kitchen, living room and dining area. It also had a private entrance, basement, and garage. Privacy is what she needed.

Her wedding rings were a problem for her. She had always worn them so she didn't think it wise to leave them behind. They were worth a small fortune; but she didn't want to draw attention to herself by trying to sell them, so she wrapped them carefully in plastic wrap and pushed them down into a jar of cold cream. That was all she could think of to do with them.

Within the week, as promised, Mrs. C called and informed her that she would like to meet with her once more to go over a few things, as she was sure she would be hired. Elated at the prospect of fulfilling work again, she was still uneasy. She knew how close people sometimes became when they worked together day after day. She would have to be cautious and careful of everything she said.

She returned to the center and was hired to work full-time, Monday through Friday, from seven in the morning until three-thirty in the afternoon. There were three other women who took care of the children: Anne, Pamela and Janice. Mrs. C and Pamela opened the center at six o'clock in the morning, arriving a little before six to start the coffee and get ready for the day. Anne started at seven, as would Laura. Janice worked from nine to six o'clock in the evening, when they closed. It seemed that Mrs. C was there from six to six. She managed the center, and it ran like an expensive watch. She was a kind woman, but dressed in a business suit and didn't actually take care of the children. She was very strict, however, about the care given, and the center was touted as the best in the area. She was very proud of that.

And then there was Flora, a very large black woman, who kept the place clean and orderly. The children loved her and often would curl up on her lap and snuggle into her soft bosom. Black and white alike, they all loved her and the feeling was mutual. Flora moved at one speed, which was slow, but somehow she managed to keep up with all her duties. The kitchen and utility rooms were spotless, and the linens on the cribs and napping cots were always fresh and clean. The play area was tidy too, but she always found the time to help a toddler with a puzzle or rock a baby to sleep. She even made special treats for them in the small kitchen, making a point of learning their favorites from their mothers. Laura was taken with this woman from the first day she worked with her.

"You sho' don't look like no California girl, Miz Holt," Flora told her as they worked together in the kitchen one morning. Laura had told her that she lived there before moving to the Midwest.

"I don't? What do you think I look like, Flora?" she asked.

"I think you looks like a troubled girl, Miz Holt," she answered.

"Flora, I wish you would call me Laura. We've worked together for six months now. We don't have to be formal, do we?" Then trying to get off the subject of her troubles, she asked, "Flora, do you have any kids?"

Flora leaned her head back against the cupboard door and closed her eyes. "I had two boys long time ago. Now I have one," she said.

"I'm sorry, Flora. I didn't mean to pry," Laura said softly.

"Oh, shucks. That's awright. It was a long time ago. Twenty years now. Yes-m, twenty years." Laura didn't know if she should ask more or not, but Flora told her. It seems she had two little sons, ages six and four. They were playing with a new bat and ball in the front yard of their home when the older boy chased the ball into the street, and was hit by a car.

"He died that night in the hospital," Flora said, wiping her eyes. "Massive head injuries, the doctor said. Some pains don't never go away, and that's fo' sho'."

"I'm so sorry, Flora. That must have been awful for you," she said, not really knowing, never having had a child of her own.

"I was all alone then too," Flora continued. "Their daddy walked out jus' before James was born. Leonard was the oldest. Now that's the bad part. The good part is James is in medical school and doing real good. I'll be working 'til I'm a hundred, I think," she smiled, as though she didn't mind at all doing that for her son.

"Couldn't he get loans?" Laura asked.

"Ah shucks, he gots loans, but I don't want him to have to work too. He gots the best grades, and I don't think he could if he had to work."

The talk of head injuries and doctors made Laura's palms sweat. She excused herself and took the bottles to the babies.

~11~

"Bless me, Father, for I have sinned," she whispered, quietly into the black screen of the confessional booth. She simply could not get rid of the guilt for what she had done. She'd had a Catholic friend in high school and went to the church with her once for confession at Easter time. Of course, she sat in the pew and waited for her friend, but they had talked about it a bit afterward as she was curious.

She had watched as the people came out of the confessional with their heads bowed, some having a look of true remorse on their faces. They would kneel and pray awhile and then leave the darkened church. Outside of the church she had seen these same people smiling and chatting with friends, looking as though they had been relieved of a burden. That was what she needed now, to be relieved.

"How long has it been since your last confession?" the priest asked.

"I've never been before. I'm not of the faith, Father," she replied.

He told her to go ahead and she did. She told

him everything, knowing that he was sworn to secrecy in his position. When she finished, he was silent for quite awhile. He had never heard a confession like this in all his years as a priest. He would not take it lightly, and took his time in answering. She almost got up and left, but then he proceeded. He asked a few questions, which she answered honestly. Then he spoke to her at great length with quietly measured words. She listened carefully. He finished by saying,

"The only thing I can tell you, my child, is that you must turn yourself in to the authorities at once. That is my answer, and I will pray for you; but I cannot forgive this deed in good conscience. Justice must be served. Now go in peace." She heard him mumble something as she left the confessional and hurried out of the church, not wanting him to have a chance to see her.

Well, that surely didn't help. She felt no better and went home. She was struggling almost every day now with what she had done and couldn't get it out of her mind. Had she really thought she would be able to? Take a human life, and then get it out of her head? She hadn't thought at all. Why hadn't she just disappeared, but left Robert there alive? Oh, the questions she asked herself, and the regrets she had - she would surely drive herself insane.

Laura was most comfortable while at work. She loved the kids and got along well with women who worked with her. Pamela was the oldest of the three women and worked closely with Mrs. C. Anne was quite young and went to night school. Janice was somewhcre in between the two in age, and was the mother of grown children.

Laura had little in common with any of them, but got along well. Oddly, she felt closest to Flora. She would often watch her as they worked. She admired her a lot. Flora was Flora; what you saw was what you got. She had nothing to hide and was comfortable with herself. She was kind and loving to everyone.

At times Laura would think of telling Flora about her past, but knew it wouldn't be fair to burden her in that way; and it would, indeed, be a burden. Flora was a religious woman and a regular at the Baptist Church in town. Laura wondered what her friend would think of her if she knew.

~~~

Three years had passed since Laura started working at the day-care center, and she loved it more each day. She longed for a child of her own, but knew that was impossible. She could never marry someone without telling him of her past, and that would surely scarc off any man. She didn't think she really deserved to be completely happy anyway because of what she had done, but she had this need to love and be loved.

One morning as Laura was setting up the play area for bowling, one of the girls told her that her cat had kittens the night before.

"Mabel, she's our cat, you know, and she had six babies in the kitchen last night," Megan announced. "And our mom let me and my brothers watch!" Megan was four years old and very mature for her age.
~~~

"Really?" Laura asked. She certainly had never witnessed a birth of any kind. "What was it like?" she asked the little girl.

"Well, there was some blood and water stuff and the babies were all inside something like a bag or something, and Mabel had to lick them all off with her tongue to clean them and then they cried and she licked them more. My brothers said it was gross, but I didn't think so. When they got all dry, they drank milk from Mabel's stomach and went to sleep. Mom says in a few days we can pick them up maybe, but not now 'cause they're too small and we could hurt them, she said. Maybe I could bring them here when they're bigger and show everyone. Do you think I could, Miss-us Hoat?" She couldn't seem to get the "l" in Holt.

"Well, we'll have to wait and see, Megan, but I think it would be nice. We would have to ask Mrs. C, of course." The other children were rounded up and the bowling began.

Ten days later, Megan dashed into the building, barely saying good-bye to her mother.

"Miss-us Hoat!" she called, looking for Laura, who was in the kitchen, but heard the little girl clearly.

"Hi, Megan, what's up?" she asked, walking towards her to help with her coat.

"Two of the babies have open eyes!"

"No!"

"Uh-huh, yes they do - two do!" Laura got down on one knee.

"Your zipper is stuck, Megan. Let's see if I can fix it for you," she said.

"What color are their eyes?" she asked.

Megan put her fingers to her lips and squeezed her eyes shut, then opened them wide and said, "Blue!"

Laura got the zipper down and helped her out of her coat. The little girl put her arms around Laura's neck and whispered into her hair, "I love you, Miss-us Hoat."

Laura felt her throat tighten and a tear stung her eye. "I love you too, Megan, and I'm happy about your kittens," she said.

Megan let go of her grip on Laura and looked her straight in the eye.

"Want one? Mom says we can give them to nice people when they're bigger. You could have one - you're nice. Want one?"

"Thank you. I'll think about it, Sweetheart," Laura answered, nose to nose with Megan.

That night, Laura was awake long after she turned out the light. She could still feel Megan's little arms around her neck. She let the tears flow, not even trying to stop them. How could she have come to this? She regretted everything she had done. Why hadn't she thought more about it? Oh, she had thought about it a lot. Her murder plan was perfectly orchestrated and carried out, but how had she not understood the value of a human life - this wonderful gift we have been given to do with what we wish. Had she thought about that?

She had learned more in the few years since the murder than all those before. How could it be? Her parents had taken care of her, but they had never impressed on her the importance of *life* or a sense of values. They just sort of glided through life, and if they understood it, they never conveyed it to their daughter; or had they tried and she wasn't listening? She didn't blame her parents at all for the deed she had done, but how was it that she had learned more from others than from them? Aren't parents suppose to teach their children to love and respect themselves and other people? And to do what's right even if it's not the easiest thing to do, or the most popular trend at the time? She was learning these things now as an adult, and much of it from the kids she cared for. She felt, at this point, that she had actually taken two lives; Robert's and her own, for she could never have a real life.

"What happened to you, Robert?" she said aloud to no one. "Why did you change so . . .?" She wondered silently if he had been gay. Why had he married her in the first place? They only had a few months of real happiness. She would never understand.

"Maybe I should turn myself in," she whispered to the darkened room and cried herself to sleep.

~12~

Back at Community General, talk of the murder had died down. Once in awhile Dr. Tulley's name would come up in conversation, and the employees, who had known him, would explain what happened to the new people. It was the biggest mystery in town, and there were still no clues to Mrs. Tulley's whereabouts.

At Police Headquarters the file sat on a shelf, collecting dust. It wasn't closed however, as there is no statute of limitations for a homicide. As far as Detective Dawson was concerned, the case was cold, but not forgotten. It still haunted him every day of his life.

On a whim, he had taken the afghan out of the dusty evidence box and brought it over to forensics, where one of his old friends worked.

"Wally. Could you do me a favor?" he asked.

"You bet. What have you got?" his friend answered, always happy to help.

"Remember the Tulley case? It's been three years now and I just can't let it go. Would you check this blanket for blood? It's just a hunch, but what the hell." Why had he bagged the afghan in the first place? He never really knew, but always thought the crime scene seemed staged. Now he had a feeling, just a feeling, and he told no one but Wally.

"You're really hooked on this thing, aren't you?" his friend asked him. "Why can't you just forget it?"

"That's what my wife keeps asking me. I try not to talk about it anymore, but it's driving me crazy."

"Well, I'll give you a call when I have the results. Won't take long," Wally told him.

Luminol, the invisible blood reagent, revealed minuscule blood stains on the fringe of the afghan. Very tiny, as she had been so careful, but enough there to do DNA testing.

Wally called his friend with the results. The blood on the afghan belonged to Robert Tulley. Dawson rubbed his chin . . . could have splattered, he thought. The blows had been hard, but Wally said that the tiny stains were smeared as though the blanket had been moved, or rearranged some way before the blood dried. He remembered that the couch the afghan had been placed on was quite a distance from the body. Not impossible, but he had another idea. What if someone had carefully covered the body while they prepared the scene, so they didn't have to look at the body and its devastation? Fibers from the afghan had been found on the victim's clothing. He remembered that now too. He was deep in thought when the phone on his desk rang and brought him back to the present. "Detective Dawson here . . . ."

~~~
~~~

Laura was helping the kids pick up the crayons and return them to the proper boxes when Flora had to raise her voice to get her attention.

"Laura! Miz Holt, can you hear me?" she asked.

"Oh, Flora. I didn't hear you. I'm sorry. What did you say?"

"Didn't hear me? You was in another world, girl. I said, Megan's mother is looking to talk to you. She's waiting up by the door," Flora said, shaking her head as she walked away thinking something was up with that girl. She hadn't been herself lately.

Laura left the play area and went to the front door where Megan's mother waited.

"Hello, Mrs. Redmon. How may I help you?"

"Hi, Laura. Megan told me that you said she could possibly bring the kittens in sometime to show the kids. Have you thought any more about it? They're big enough now and very playful. It would be fun."

Laura hadn't asked Mrs. C as yet, but told Megan's mom that she would ask today and let her know in the morning. "I think the kids would love that," she told her. "Megan has kept me up to date on their development, I can tell you," she said laughing.

"Oh, I'm sure she has. This is the biggest news we've had at our house in quite some time. Megan said you may want one, is that right? Or does she just want you to take one?"

"She did offer me one, but I haven't given it too much thought. Maybe seeing them will help me decide. I'll let you know tomorrow, if it's okay. And thank you for thinking of the kids."

She had been lost in thought, or in another world, as Flora said. She was consumed with thoughts of Robert; what she had done to him and more importantly what she was going to do about it. She could not go on forever like this. She knew now that seldom was there reason to justify taking the life of another human being. Self defense was all she could come up with, and that had not been the case. Why hadn't she just left him? She had been gone for three years now and no one had found her. She could have had a life.

~~~

Permission was granted that the little cat family would visit on Friday. Megan could hardly wait for the week to pass. When Friday finally arrived, she and her mother came a little early with the cats in a cardboard box that was lined with a blanket. The meowing could be heard as soon as they entered the building.

"They just do that," Megan announced. "There's nothing wrong. They want to get out of the box," she explained to the women with much authority in her voice.

It was decided that the children would sit in a circle on the rug in the play area with the kittens in the center. Mabel was a bit nervous at first, but made no attempt to move her babies. They were almost old enough now to leave her, so she sat and watched them from outside the circle.

It was great fun! The kids rolled little balls and watched the kittens chase them, do somersaults and wrestle with each other. Laura watched as the kids got breathless with laughter. This had been a very
~~~

good idea. Even LeRoy was joining in the fun. He was a quiet little boy with a shock of red hair and a face covered with freckles. If that wasn't enough, his ears protruded out from his head like handles on a pitcher. Every now and then one of the other kids would tease him about his looks and he would cry. It was Flora who usually stepped in and put an end to that. She never made it seem like she was protecting him though, she would simply ask him to do a favor for her. By the time he had fetched what she needed, the other kids forgot about the teasing and LeRoy was distracted enough to stop crying.

But today he wasn't crying at all. He was enthralled with the antics of the kittens. Laura sat next to him on the floor, and wiggling her finger on the carpet, caught the attention of one of the cats. The kitten ran to her and attacked her finger, while LeRoy laughed with delight. She scooped up the kitten in her arms and began to pet it. Soon the purring began and the little animal settled down. LeRoy watched her every move and smiled at her. She carefully placed the kitten in his lap and watched as his little face lit up.

"Have you ever held a kitten, LeRoy?" she asked him. He shook his head and grinned. No, he never had.

Mrs. C, hearing the laughter, came out of her office and watched the action. How sweet it was to watch precious little children interact with animals, she thought. We must do this again.

In time the kittens tired of playing and gathered together in a pile with their mother for a nap.

It was time for the morning snack, so the children left them alone. There was a hush in the room. The children were aware of the sleeping animals and ate their crackers and drank their juice quietly.

When Laura got home from work, she was still smiling. Today had been such fun. She was seriously considering taking one of the kittens. She shared the duplex she lived in with the landlady; and when she saw her come home from work, she asked her if pets were allowed.

"Well, like what? Not a Rottweiler, I hope," the woman answered.

"Oh, no. Nothing like that. I was thinking of a kitten, and I wanted to ask first," Laura told her.

"Cats are okay; but if they damage the carpet in there, or scratch the woodwork, you'll be held responsible. I actually like them myself," she added. "I have one, but you've probably never seen him. He doesn't go out anymore. He's getting too old."

"I didn't know you had a cat," Laura said. How on earth would she? She had only spoken to this women a few times since she moved into the duplex. She always put the rent check under her door in the back hallway and rarely saw her.

Well, now she had something to think about; something upbeat for a change. It made her feel good. She didn't know very much about cats, but thought she could learn and would be grateful for the company. She had led a very solitary life for quite awhile. She wondered how long cats lived - maybe she shouldn't take on a responsibility if she wouldn't be around to carry it out. Oh, the regrets she had.

Monday morning, the talk at the day-care center

was all about kittens. The younger children, who couldn't talk yet, just grinned as they understood what the older kids were jabbering about. Two of them thought that their mothers would let them adopt a kitten; so they were envied by the others, and plans were in the works for more pets to be brought in as it had been such a success. Laura was still thinking about it and Megan was helping her decide.

"Which one do you want, Miss-us Hoat?" she would ask several times a day. "You better hurry, else they'll be all gone!" she would tell her. Three days later, Laura made up her mind. She would take a kitten, and she wanted a female. Megan picked out the prettiest girl kitten for her. A small gray and white tiger with sapphire blue eyes. Laura named her Mabelina after Mabel, the mother cat. Megan thought it was a very nice name, and told Mabel all about it later.

~13~

How could something so small bring so much joy to a person? Laura was falling in love with the kitten and the feeling was mutual. They were together every moment that Laura was home. The cat was in her lap in the evening and at the foot of her bed at night. She even sat on the edge of the tub when Laura bathed. She couldn't imagine being alone now, and wondered how she had lived without this warm ball of fur with a beating heart. She had been more lonely than she realized.

In all this time, she had only gone out on a date once. Well, it wasn't really a date; she didn't have the nerve for that kind of thing. Janice, the woman she worked with at the day-care center, invited her to go out for dinner and dancing one weekend when her single brother was visiting from out of town. Laura had hesitated at first; but then thought about it and decided if he lived in another state, it couldn't lead to anything. So she agreed. It proved to be a great evening. Thomas was a good dancer; and Janice and her husband knew a place where the band played the kind of music they all liked. It had been a very long time since Laura danced. Thomas was a nice man, maybe not exactly what she would choose, no sparks flew between them, but she'd had such fun. She was missing so much, but knew she could have no more. Ah, the regrets . . . .

~~~

"Miss-us Hoat!" Megan said, in a raised voice. "How is Mabel-eena?"

"She's just fine, Megan. Why do you ask?" They were cleaning up after lunch.

"Well, I want to know if she's okay, or if she's any trouble," she said seriously. All the kittens were adopted now and Megan felt a bit lost. She had taken such pride in helping Mabel with her first litter.

"She's fine, Sweetheart. And how is Mabel?" Laura asked.

"Well, she seems okay, but I think she misses her babies a lot," she said, hanging her head. Laura gave her a hug and thanked her for helping clean up. Laura loved this little girl. Well, she loved them all, but this one was special and now they were even more connected because of the cats.

Two of the children in day-care had taken a kitten as well. Megan was asking Alex how his kitten was doing. She was quite the mother hen, Laura thought.

"He's good," Alex told her, "and fast as lightning, I can't even catch him!" Megan laughed at that and went to ask the girl who had a kitten too. It seems they were all doing fine and were happy in their new homes.

That evening, after supper, Laura sat with the
~~~

cat in her lap and did some serious thinking. She couldn't go on this way, but wasn't sure what to do. She thought of all the wonderful people she knew from the day-care, especially the children. What would they think of her? What would Flora think? She was a different person now and at times, couldn't believe what she had done. It seemed as though she had watched someone else do the deed. More mature now, she knew that somehow she could have gotten away from Robert and had a chance at life; maybe a husband, a home and children of her own. She began to cry and stroke the ever-present cat in her lap.

"What shall I do, Mabelina?" she asked. "Whatever shall I do?" She pushed it to the back of her mind, and tried to concentrate on her job and everyday life in general. At times she actually forgot her past entirely during the day, but it haunted her in the evenings when she was alone with the cat.

~~~

She was able to carry on this charade for two more years. She actually had a life and was enjoying it. Mabelina was an adult now, and the kids at the day-care were different. All of the children that she had started out caring for were now gone and in school. She was living a lie and denying it everyday. Lately though, for some reason, her conscience seemed to be in over-drive.

~~~

Meanwhile, back home, Detective Dawson was still sifting through the evidence and questioning people who knew the couple. Many had been questioned right after the murder, but he was digging even deeper now. He was beginning to put the pieces together. He was pretty sure that the wife was the perpetrator and assumed that she had taken the murder weapon with her when she disappeared. But where was she?

He learned that Marian had not wanted to leave her job at the hospital, but did so for her husband. She also desperately wanted a child of her own. After talking with many of the doctors once again, he was told by Dr. William Green that a vasectomy had been performed on Robert. Why would a man have that done if his wife wanted so badly to have a child? He was learning much more about this man they had called the "Golden Boy." He couldn't explain to anyone why he was so compelled to solve this case and did the investigating on his own time. He always did love a mystery. Well, wasn't that why he had chosen police work for a career? This one was driving him crazy though; it really was. He had a few more things to go over and then would ask the chief about putting a spot on the television show, "America's Most Wanted" or maybe "Unsolved Mysteries." He knew the success both of the shows had in finding people. It was a long shot, but he had exhausted most other ideas.

~14~

She had just poured coffee for the officers sitting at her kitchen table when the phone rang. She lifted the receiver and said, "Hello." No one answered. She repeated it again and again, but no one spoke and the phone wouldn't stop ringing.

Then she woke and sat straight up in bed, startling the cat. She hit the alarm button with her palm and gathered Mabelina into her lap. Her heart raced and she was sweating. It was a *dream!* She dreamed they had found her. Sliding back down under the covers, she pulled the cat up to her chest and tried to slow down her breathing; a whisker brushed her face.

Laura closed her eyes and stroked the cat, she was sure now what she must do. She would have to plan carefully, the way she had planned the murder; and there must be a way to keep the day-care out of this. It would certainly destroy the sterling reputation that Mrs. C had earned, if it was known that a murderer had been caring for the children. She could not allow that to happen. After spending a few minutes petting the cat, she threw back the covers and headed for the shower. She had to be at work in forty-five minutes.

"Good morning!" she said to all, as cheerfully as she could, when she got to work. Some of the children were already busy coloring at the table, while others were just arriving. Laura went back to put her purse in the locker and nearly bumped into Flora on the way.

"Oh, Miz Laura! Sorry . . . you okay?" Flora was carrying a stack of folded sheets that nearly blocked her view, and Laura, deep in thought, wasn't paying attention.

"Flora! You startled me. I didn't see you," she said, with as much composure as she could muster. Her mind was racing, and she could still feel the physical effects of the dream. "I guess I was daydreaming - sorry, Flora," she said smiling.

"You been doing lots of that lately, seems to me!" Flora told her as she put the sheets away in the linen closet. "Everything okay? Anything you want to talk about? I be lis'ning, you knows that."

Oh, if only she could talk to Flora, but no, she couldn't. "I know that, Flora, and I thank you. Now I'd better get to work."

Laura tried to concentrate on what she was doing as best she could, but her mind wouldn't stop planning. When three o'clock rolled around, she welcomed it. Her plan was beginning to take shape, and her head was whirling with thoughts.

That evening she sat at the kitchen table with paper and pencil, trying to organize her thoughts. The cat was lying on the newspaper next to her, following every movement of the pencil with her eyes.

"You know you're not supposed to be on the table, Mabelina," she said, putting her head next to the cat so she could rub against her. "What am I going to do about you, my friend?" She scratched her under her chin, and the cat purred. Laura thought about her landlady whose very old cat must have died by now and added, ask Mrs. Kline about the cat, to her list of things to do. "I'll miss you, sweet girl," she said quietly.

She thought that she would need a month to accomplish each item on the list. There was much to do: bank accounts, apartment, car, furniture, and so on. She made herself a cup of tea and sipped it slowly as she read over the things she had written. The cat dozed peacefully on the newspaper. Laura picked up the pencil and wrote down Flora's name. She thought that her friend would be able to help her protect the day-care center. "What will she think?" she whispered to no one.

She had quite a bit of money that she wouldn't need where she was going and it occurred to her that she had always had more than enough. Even as a child, anything she asked for her parents bought for her. She saw how some people struggled from paycheck to paycheck and she felt even guiltier. She'd had so much, and messed up so badly . . . .

Her plan was taking shape nicely. She had thought of everything and now felt relieved. She remembered what the priest told her when she had gone to confession. "The only thing I can tell you, my child, is that you must turn yourself in to the authorities. I will pray for you . . . now go in peace."

"Thank you, Father," she whispered, wishing she

was a more religious person.

How would she be able to go back to being Marian Tulley, she wondered. She felt as though she was two separate people and liked being Laura Holt much better than the former. But, because she was Laura Holt and had learned so much as that person, she knew she must go back and do what was right. She wished that she could somehow tell his parents just how sorry she was, but knew that nothing would bring back their only son. Ah . . . regrets.

~~~

She knocked on her landlady's back door and clasped her hands behind her back, trying to stay calm. This was the first item on her to-do list. When she heard footsteps approaching, she stood up straight and put on her best smile. The door opened.

"Hi, Mrs. Kline. I wonder if I could talk to you for a few minutes. Is this a good time?" she asked politely.

"Sure, it's fine. Is there something wrong in your apartment? Come in! Come in and sit down."

"Thank you, Mrs. Kline, I . . ."

"Call me Rita - please. Come on now, sit down. Want a cup of coffee?" Laura told her she would and wished she had gotten to know this woman a little better, forgetting how frightened she'd been of everyone when she arrived here.

"So what's wrong over there? Nothing that can't be fixed, I'm sure," Rita said, hoping it wouldn't be too expensive.

"Nothing's wrong. I love the place, but I have to move back home. Ah . . . due to a family illness," she said, keeping her voice steady.
~~~

"Oh, I'm sorry to hear that. How soon do you have to leave?" Rita asked, thinking about the lease that Laura had signed.

"I need to go as soon as possible. I'll give two weeks notice at work, but I wanted to talk to you first about a few things."

"Okay, like what? Want some cream for your coffee?" Laura shook her head and took a sip from the steaming mug.

"First of all, I know I still have months to go on my lease, and I'll pay that in full. Then there's the cat . . . yours must be gone now, right?" Rita nodded sadly.

"I can't take Mabelina with me," Laura said. "I need to find her a good home. She's good and very affectionate. Would you be interested in taking her?"

Rita rubbed her bottom lip with her forefinger and smiled. "You know, this is weird, I've been thinking about getting a cat a lot lately; I just might take her. Course I'd have to see her first before I make up my mind for sure," she said.

"Of course," Laura said, and continued. "Then there's the furniture in my place. It's like new and I can't take that either. I would gladly give it to you, or you could leave it and rent the apartment furnished."

"Get a moving van, why don't you? They'll do everything - even pack for you," Rita offered.

"I really can't do that. I'll be living in a place that's furnished. Don't feel like you have to take it. I just wanted to give you first chance. I'll give it to the Goodwill Charities if you don't want it. Would you like to go over and see it?" she asked, grateful that Rita wasn't asking too many questions.

"Yes, let's do that. I'd like to see everything! Some of my stuff is older than dirt - yes, let's go," she said, putting the empty cups into the sink.

"You can see Mabelina too," she smiled. "Her mother's name is Mabel, so that's why I call her that."

Rita gave her a sideways grin, and told her that she liked the name.

The two women spent over an hour at Laura's place that afternoon. Rita and the cat made friends quickly and it was decided that she would donate *her* furnishings to charity and keep Laura's. She couldn't believe her luck. "How is it that we never got to know each other?" Rita asked as she was leaving. "You've been a great tenant; no trouble at all and no noise, but I wish you had come over to visit a long time ago. I really do, and I hope everything works out for you back home."

"Thank you, Rita, for everything. I'll talk to you soon. If you'd like, you could keep the cat overnight sometime to see how you get along," she suggested.

"That's a good idea. I'll let you know," she said and went back to her own apartment.

"Whew," Laura whistled softly after the door was closed. "That went well." Her plans were in motion and she felt better already.

~15~

It was Saturday and she was ready. She gave two weeks notice at the day-care center, and Wednesday had been her last day. She sold her car, closed her bank accounts, and said good-bye to Rita. The hardest part so far had been letting Mabelina go. The thought of being locked up wouldn't be so bad, if she could have the cat with her. She felt so alone and brushed away a tear as she remembered how she and Rita had pushed and shoved her furniture through the back hall into the other apartment. Mabelina had such fun running between the two apartments while the door was propped open. Laura was sure that she would be happy with Rita, but it had been hard to say good-bye.

Rita was out for the evening playing bingo with her sister; she would be home late. Laura had taken this time to color her hair dark brown as it was before. She had let it grow out a bit so she looked like her old self again.

"Marian. Marian Tulley," she said to herself in the mirror. "My, how you've changed!"

She sat on the floor as she went over her list one

more time. She had destroyed all identification and any papers referring to Laura Holt. Her main objective was to protect the day-care center. She wasn't sure that she could do it though. But why would anyone need to know where she had been, if she turned herself in? She wondered about that a lot.

With her list nearly completed, she got up and took the last can of soda out of the fridge, now it was empty. The whole place was empty and clean. It was ready to rent again. There would be no hurry though, as she had paid her lease in full and added quite a bit extra for Mabelina's care.

Sitting on the floor, she pulled her small suitcase next to her so she could use it to write on. She wrote a short note to Rita, thanking her again for all she had done, and then she wrote a letter to Flora. She needed to explain things to her friend. It was only three days ago that she had said good-bye, but it seemed longer. Flora had cried.

"You take care now, girl, and write to us when you gets to California, you hear?" She wiped her eyes and blew her nose hard. "I'm gonna miss you, Miz Laura. Things won't be the same around here, that's fo' sho'."

It was then that she had pressed the jar of cold cream into Flora's hand. Flora looked confused and started to speak.

Laura shook her head and put her finger to her lips. "Shhh, Flora," she said. "Remember when you said you were having trouble with your skin"? she fudged, just in case someone was within earshot. "This will help." Flora's mouth opened again, but she covered the jar with her other hand and didn't say a word.

"Keep it safe, Flora. I'll write to you soon and explain," she told her. Oh, how was she ever going to explain her past life in a letter? She took her time writing, and when she finished, read it over carefully. She had told the truth. She hoped Flora could forgive her. She addressed the envelope and put on a stamp. She was ready - it was time to go. Once again, she would leave her home under the cloak of darkness, but this time it was very different.

She stood in the darkened apartment and watched for the cab through the half-opened blinds. When the headlights approached, she took one last look around the place that she had called home for five years and closed the blinds. She put the keys on the kitchen counter and left through the front door, pushing the lock button on the way out.

She rode in the taxicab to the bus station in silence. The driver asked where she was going and said no more; she was grateful for that.

There were several people in the bus station when she arrived. This time she knew where she was going and had called for information before she left home. She purchased a ticket and found a place to sit down. There would be a twenty-minute wait. As before, she had a book to read, thus avoiding conversation with anyone waiting with her. When the bus pulled into the station, she gathered her things and boarded along with the other travelers. Finding a window seat, she sat down and pressed her head against the glass. If only she could go back in time, she could have thought of a way to leave Robert. Oh, the regrets she has.

~16~

Flora hauled herself up the front steps of her home after work, checking the mailbox as she always did before going inside. She dropped her coat and purse on the chair in the front hall and made her way to the kitchen, shuffling through the mail as she walked. "Light bill, junk mail, mo' junk," she said to no one. "What's this?" It was a pretty blue envelope addressed in a beautiful script. She sat at the kitchen table and opened the letter with a butter knife that she kept there just for that purpose. The envelope was thick, as the letter was long. *Dear Flora,* it began. *By the time you receive this I will be at my destination, and doing what I should have done long ago.*

She read slowly and carefully, not wanting to miss a word. "Lord av' mercy," she breathed, as she shifted to a more comfortable position. She couldn't believe what she was reading. How on earth could this woman, whom she had grown so close to, have done what this letter said? Flora felt as though she had been deceived, and she didn't like the feeling one bit. She brushed away a tear and continued reading.

My main concern, now, is to protect the day-care center. I need your help with this, Flora, she read. She had to admit that Laura or Marian, whoever she was, intended to do the right thing, now.

"But, shucks, that don't bring nobody dead back," Flora said aloud. She closed her eyes and asked the Lord for help. The answer came to her quickly. As long as Laura was turning herself into the police, Flora would help her protect the day-care center. She picked up the letter and continued to read. *You'll find my rings in the bottom of the cold cream jar, Flora. I want you to have them.* Flora pushed back her chair and went to her bedroom, leaving the letter where it lay. The cold cream jar was in the top drawer of her dresser. She opened it and stuck her finger into the cream. She felt something hard. When she had cleaned off her finger and unwrapped the rings, she went back to the kitchen and sat down once more. She couldn't believe her eyes. The rings were stunning. The center diamond was bigger than any she had ever seen, at least on anyone she knew. "My, my," she whispered. There were many stones surrounding the large one, and the wedding band was encrusted with diamonds as well. She slipped them onto her little finger and held the letter close to her chest. It was then that she began to cry. This Laura/Marian was a good and decent person, as far as Flora knew. Something awful must have happened to make her commit this crime. She hadn't said much about that part in the letter, and took full blame for her actions. Oh, if Flora could just put her big arms around her now and hold her. "Oh, Miz Laura," she said, and blew her nose. She finished reading the letter and was saddened by the ending, but understood Laura's reasoning.

We will never be able to correspond again, Flora. All my mail from this point on will be screened. We can't take the chance of anyone knowing I was connected with the day-care center. It would mean its ruin, and I can't let that happen. Flora shook her head and finished reading the letter.

Thank you, Flora, for being so kind to me. I felt proud to call you my friend. You are indeed an inspiration, and I will never forget you. Yours truly, Laura.

Flora tried to hold back the tears, but couldn't. She was touched by what Laura had said about her being an inspiration. She had never thought of herself that way. She had just always tried to do the right thing. She was still crying as she took the rings and the letter to her room and buried them in a drawer under her sweaters. She would have to do some hard thinking about this. Like Laura, she didn't want anything to harm the good name of the place where she worked either. She would help, somehow.

~~~

A short time later at the day-care center, Mrs. C announced to everyone that she had recently received a generous anonymous cash donation. The donor had written that it should be used for whatever was needed for the children. She also said that never in all the time she had been working, had they received such a large sum of money. "We will be able to
~~~

afford all the things that we need," she said. "And we won't have to raise our fee. Isn't that wonderful?" Everyone agreed - it was wonderful.

Flora turned back to her work with a smile on her face, knowing full well who had left that money at the door of the center. "Bless you, Miz Laura," she said softly.

A week later, Flora told everyone at the center that she had received a letter from Laura. "She say she likes being back in California, but she misses us all. Oh, and her relative is still *very* sick," she added.

~17~

Detective Dawson was at his desk hurriedly making notes on a recent homicide. He planned to go out and question some of the employees in the work place of the suspect. He had, for the time being, put the Tulley murder out of his thoughts as he was busy with other new cases. He removed his reading glasses and placed them in his shirt pocket. Gathering his notes, he pushed back his chair and started to get up, when one of the rookie cops approached his desk.

"Detective Dawson? There's someone out in the hall who wants to speak with a detective about an old murder case."

"Show him in please," he said, as he checked his watch, and sat down.

"It's a she, Sir."

"All right, Jensen, show *her* in." He wanted to add - stop wasting my time, but didn't. These people were usually nut cases who, for lack of anything better to do, liked to conjure up scenarios about old cases they once read about in the newspaper.

Placing a paperweight on his notes, he put his

glasses back on and waited. He watched as a pretty woman walked toward the desk where he sat. When she got closer, a chill went up his spine. He was looking into the face of Marian Tulley. His heart rate sped up and he tried to keep his mouth from dropping open. He stood and wondered if he should call her by name, as she put out her hand.

"My name is Marian Tulley. I need to talk to someone about the murder of my husband." That face was emblazoned in his mind; he would never forget it. Her picture had been on the front page of every newspaper in seven surrounding counties five years before. He could barely speak as he clasped her hand in his.

"I'm Detective Dawson, Mrs. Tulley. Please sit down," he said, and then thought that they would be able to talk more privately in the interrogation room down the hall.

"Better yet, let's go down the hall, where you'll be more comfortable," he suggested, and said, "No calls," to anyone who was listening. "Would you care for some coffee?" he asked. She shook her head no, and followed him into the room. When they were seated at the long table, he cleared his throat and asked her what was on her mind. He thought he knew, but he wanted to hear it from her.

"I know every detail about my husband's murder, because I did it," she began. "I'll tell you everything with one exception."

"And what is that?" he asked, more curious than ever.

"Where I've been for the last five years."

"Well, I don't know if I can promise you anything, Mrs. Tulley," he said, rubbing his chin.

"It's imperative that no one know. It would damage the people that I worked with for five years. I cannot let that happen. I've done enough damage," she said soberly.

"Do you have legal counsel, Ma'am?"

"No, I don't need an attorney."

"You'll have to be represented, Mrs. Tulley. Even though you haven't been arrested, you have the right to remain silent. Anything you say, can and will be used . . ."

"I understand my rights, Detective. I am here to confess to the crime. All I ask is that you protect where I've been for the past five years. Do *you* understand?" she asked quietly.

"I'm not sure that I do, Ma'am. You're telling me that you murdered your husband in cold blood, and now you're here to confess?"

"That's what I'm saying."

"You do know that you could go to prison for the rest of your life, or worse, don't you? Murder one carries a sentence of 20 to 60 years - sometimes the death penalty. If you have an attorney, there's chance of a lesser charge - maybe manslaughter. If there was abuse . . . maybe self defense."

She leaned towards him and spoke softly. "I took a life, and have spent five years agonizing over it. I know what I have to do."

He couldn't believe what he was hearing. Never in all his years of law enforcement had he heard anything like this. He took a pen and a pad of paper from the table drawer and turned on the tape recorder.

"Begin anytime that you're ready," he told her.

She proceeded with her tale of murder, much as she had done in the confessional years before. She left out nothing. When he stopped her to ask a question, she would quietly answer and then continue where she had left off. She was poised, calm and articulate.

". . . then I left my house and got on a bus. I went to another city, found an apartment and a job. I had a pretty good life, but I could no longer go on with it. I think I should pay for what I did."

He sat and stared at her for a moment or two. He would help this woman any way he could, he knew that.

"There are not enough words in all of the languages for me to say how sorry I am and how much I regret what I did. I know now that I could have done something different, but at the time, I didn't. I guess I thought that he had taken over my life, so I ended his," she said. "I ache for his parents most of all. He was their only son."

Dawson turned off the tape recorder and rapidly made notes on the legal pad. When he finished, it looked more like a child's scribble than police notes, but he could decipher every word. He read what he had written and shook his head. As horrible as it was, he had to admit, it was darn clever. They had searched diligently for the murder weapon. He smiled now, remembering that innocuous-looking roast beef on the counter in this woman's kitchen. Who would have guessed?

She watched him as he read over his notes, and wondered what he thought of her. She wished she could tell him that she was a decent person, but had made a terrible error in judgement. She wouldn't though, as she sincerely wanted to make this right, or at least as right as she could.

He wanted to know why.

"What made you take such drastic action?" he asked.

She explained as best she could, trying hard not to sound as though she was defending herself.

"I simply didn't give it enough thought," she told him.

Oh, but he thought she had. She had given it a great deal of thought and carried it out with precision.

He leaned back in his chair and crossed his arms over his chest.

"I always thought that it looked staged," he said. "Did you by any chance cover your husband's body with the afghan that was on the couch near where he was lying?"

She was stunned. She thought she had been so careful. She put her elbow on the table and rested her forehead in her hand, as if she could shield herself from his stare. She began to cry.

"I . . . I covered him so I wouldn't have to see him every time I passed him as I was getting ready to leave," she said quietly.

Just as he had thought. "I was going to ask the Captain if he thought we could run this case on one of those television shows. 'America's Most Wanted' or, what's the other one?" he hesitated. "Oh, yeah, 'Unsolved Mysteries', because I didn't think we were ever going to be able to solve this one," he said, smiling at her. "But here you are."

At the thought of that, she began to perspire. "Well, now that won't be necessary," she muttered, so grateful that she had gotten to him before that happened. The whole country would know. She looked different as Laura Holt, but not that much if someone was really paying attention.

They spent another hour going over everything she told him before he excused himself and went out to find the Captain. It was during that hour that she learned of her mother's death. She began to cry for her mother after he left the room. She should have been with her. Finding some comfort in the knowledge that her mother would not have known her anyway, she dried her eyes and waited for what was coming next.

Marian knew that her story would be on the evening news, and shuddered at the thought of what people in this town would think of the beloved Dr. Tulley's horrible wife. Folding her arms on the table, she put her head down and closed her eyes, she could think no more. Her life now, was in the hands of the court.

~18~

Several weeks later, Flora was still puzzled about what she should do with the rings, and every now and then she would take them out from under her sweaters to look at them. They had to be worth a lot of money, she knew that, and the Lord knew she could use it. It would help so much with her son's education, but she had trouble convincing herself that they belonged to her. But they did, didn't they? After much prayer and thought, she had a plan. Never before had she lied to her son about anything, but this was different, and it would benefit him as much as her.

"What do you mean you found them?" James asked his mother when she showed him the rings.

"I tol' you, I found them in the bathroom at the shopping mall," she said sharply.

"Did you report it to anyone?" he wondered.

"Shucks, no!" she said emphatically. "If I did that, they'd say, 'oh yes they sure do looks like the ones I lost jus' today,' you know they would, Son."

"You're probably right," James said, never doubting her story. "I wonder what they're worth," he mused. "When did you say you found them?"

"Well now, I've had them for a while," she started. "I found them a bit ago, but I wasn't sure what to do until I talked to you." She watched his face closely looking for signs of doubt, but saw none. Part of what she said was true, she'd had them for a while. She didn't like this lying business at all. It was against everything she stood for, but this was different, wasn't it?

"I think we'll put an ad in the paper," he told her, taking charge of the situation. "We'll say, wedding ring set found. Call and describe for return - or something like that."

"That sounds good to me," Flora said, happy to be doing something with the rings at last. The ad was in the paper for a week. Flora got two calls that sounded legitimate and one that sounded as though the caller was trying hard to come as close as possible to the description, so he could claim the rings. After no success in finding the rightful owner, James took the rings for appraisal and was astounded at their worth.

"Somebody must be real unhappy," he muttered to Flora. "How could a person lose something so valuable and not try to find them?"

"Maybe they did," his mother said. "Maybe she was just passing through our town and stopped at the mall and took them off to wash her hands and then forgot where she put them. I don't know!" Flora wasn't good at lying and felt her face get hot, but her son never noticed. "I suppose we'll sell them then, James? That's what we should do, right?"

"They belong to you now, Mother. It's up to you,"

he told her.

"That's what I'm gonna do then and we'll get rid of some of them loans you gots to pay."

"You don't have to do that," he said again. "Get something for yourself - you deserve it."

She knew exactly what she would do with the money and he wouldn't be able to talk her out of it. She would help her son. The very next day, Flora burned the tell-all letter from Laura. The secret was safe.

~~~

Meanwhile, Marian had been sentenced and placed in a women's prison. She shared a cell with another woman and was trying hard to adjust to prison life. Stella had been alone in the cell for several weeks and was eager to talk, but Marian was not. She spent much of the day, at first, lying on her bunk going over and over again in her head what she had done to get herself into this place. The guilt was overwhelming and she wondered if it would ever go away. For the first five years, after the murder, she had been busy with her job, but now she had time on her hands.

"You can't do that forever, ya know," Stella said.

"Do what?" Marian asked, sitting up and trying to get her mind in the present.

"Just lie there with your eyes shut. You've been doing it since you got here."

"I'm sorry, Stella. I just can't seem to figure out why I did what I did to get myself in here, I guess."

"Well, you don't have to be sorry. Just seems to me that you can't do that for the next twenty years or however long you'll be in." Stella sat down on
~~~

her bunk, rested her elbows on her knees, and stared at her new cell-mate. "So you admit doing what got you here? Everyone in here is innocent, don't you know that?" she said, with a wry expression on her face.

"Are you innocent, Stella?" Marian asked with concern. She was very new to prison life.

"No, I'm guilty as sin and I'd do it again in a heartbeat." They sat quietly for a moment or two and then Stella spoke up. "I shot that bastard before he killed me first, but I made the mistake of doing it before he beat the crap out of me again. I should have planned better and waited until he did. Then maybe the jury would have bought the self-defense plea. They didn't, but I'd be dead now, I know, if I hadn't shot him. Maybe one of my kids would be too," she said, shaking her head.

Marian was quiet, thinking that she had no excuse for what she had done compared to what Stella was telling her. It would take her a very long time to rid herself of the guilt, if ever. She had also been thinking about her childhood and her mother's death. Stella was a good listener, so she told her about that too.

"I'm sorry about your mother," Stella said sincerely.

"Well, the blessing there was she didn't know a thing about what got me here. She was in the advanced stages of Alzheimer's disease," Marian said softly. "I wish I could have been there for her though."

The two women talked at length that day. They were beginning to like one another, which was a good thing, as they would spend a very long time together in that small cell. Stella had taken Marian under her wing, and protected her from the horrors that took place inside these walls; they formed a unit, and she could hold her own against the most aggressive inmates, so Marian felt safe with her. When they were allowed outside, the two would sit together - sometimes talking, sometimes not. When the sun was shining, they liked to sit on the benches that lined the wall of the prison with their faces turned up, hoping to get a bit of color to their cheeks. Stella chain-smoked at these times - one cigarette after another. Smoke would billow from her nostrils and mouth as she told Marian tales of living with a wife-beater. It sounded horrible.

"Couldn't you leave?" Marian asked, and then a second later thought what a stupid question that was. Why hadn't she just left Robert?

"That's what everyone thinks and asks. It's hard to do if you have kids. The minute you say anything about getting help or leaving, these jerks threaten to take the kids, or worse. He would have done it too, I know. He was a bastard," Stella told her.

When the allotted time outside was up, all the women filed into the prison once again, passing the mail room on the way. In this room, all incoming and outgoing mail was inspected and read, and determined if it would be processed. Marian rarely slowed down as she passed the window where the mail was handed out, as she never got any.

"Stella Harmon!" the guard called. Marian and Stella were finishing a conversation they had started outside and forgotten all about the mail. Stella went to the window and mumbled her thanks. She tucked the letter in the pocket of her gray jump-suit and followed Marian back to their cell, where she lay down on her bunk and read the letter from her daughter.

Marian envied her cell-mate at these times. It would be nice to get something from the outside now and then, she thought.

Stella read the letter over and over again before she swung her legs off her bunk and sat up. "She's the only one who writes to me anymore," she told Marian. "My son still hates me and my other daughter just doesn't care, I guess."

"Doesn't your son realize what his dad was like?" Marian asked.

"He's the youngest - only eight when I . . . when his dad died." They talked about Stella's kids for a bit and then the conversation changed. Stella was amazed that Marian had turned herself in.

"I can't figure out why you would do that. I'd give anything to not be in this damn place," she said, shaking her head. Stella was in for life with no chance of parole.

"My conscience wouldn't leave me alone," Marian stated flatly. "I had a dream too. Did I ever tell you about that?"

Stella shook her head no, she hadn't told her that.

"It was the strangest thing, and so real. Two policemen came to the door and wanted to question me about something. I let them in - I had no choice, and offered them coffee. Then the phone rang and wouldn't stop. Actually it was my alarm ringing and

I woke up. It scared me so much that I began planning what to do that very day," she told her.

"Well, I think you were crazy. Who would have known? You said they were never close to finding you, didn't you? And just where were you all that time anyway?" Stella wondered.

"I told you my conscience wouldn't let me rest, and I'm sure they would have found me eventually," she said, remembering what Detective Dawson told her about putting the story on television. "I can't tell you where I was, Stella. I haven't told anyone, and I won't. I want to protect the place where I worked and the people there. It would do a lot of damage if they knew the truth about me," she said honestly.

Stella lay back down and closed her eyes. She never would have done what Marian did. Never would she have turned herself in . . . never. She was going to die in this place and she lived with that thought every day.

~19~

Prison life was an eye opener for Marian, and the longer she was there the worse she felt. She had certainly led a sheltered life. About half of the women in this particular prison were between the ages of 25 and 34, and unemployed when arrested. Many of them had never been married, and more than three-quarters of them had children. A few of the women were pregnant when arrested and delivered their babies while serving time. Over 60 percent had not finished high school, and many were incarcerated for drug offenses. How could she have done what she did after leading such a privileged life? These women came from dysfunctional homes and a lot of them had horrible upbringings. It depressed Marian, and she often dreamed of her job at the day-care center, her apartment and the cat she left behind.

Unlike Stella, Marian was pretty sure she would be out someday. She would be over fifty years old when eligible for parole in fifteen years. She was a model prisoner. She never caused a bit of trouble for anyone. At times she would day-dream about what she would do with her life then. How she longed to work again with little kids, knowing now that she would never have her own; but that seemed unlikely.

In time, Marian proved to be responsible enough to work in the prison laundry. A pretty lowly job, she had to admit, but it was something to do, and she earned a few dollars a day. It was hot as hell in the laundry center; the fans did little to circulate the heavily moistened air. The worst job of all though, was working the massive mangle for pressing. It looked as though it had come from another century it was so old. It was used mainly for pressing the sheets after they came out of the dryer. The sheets here were not what Marian was used to, for sure. They were rough and came out of the dryer badly wrinkled. Marian hated pressing sheets, not the work so much, but the horror story the other women told her when she first started working there. It was rumored that several years before, one of the inmates with a grievance against a fellow prisoner, had put her arm in the mangle and watched it go through all the way up to her elbow before the guard could get there and hit the release button. Marian was always watchful as she folded a freshly-dried sheet in half. She would place the end of it smoothly on the padded roller, then quickly pull the lever that lowered the hot steel cover to the sheet, and engaged the gears to turn the roller. She was never sure if the perspiration on her forehead was from the warm steamy room, or the thought of her arm being pulled along with the sheet.

She proved to be a good worker and was transferred, after six months, to the prison library. This work suited her much better and at times she could lose herself in a fascinating book and forget where she was for a few minutes. She was educating herself now, and thought again of the opportunity for an education that she had blown off all those years ago. Oh, if we could have a second chance at life, she lamented, as she returned books to their rightful places on the shelves; I would get an education, find the right man, marry him and have a family - two kids at least, she mused. "That is what I would do," she whispered to no one.

~~~

In ten years of prison life, Marian had received no mail and had only one visitor. Detective Dawson stopped by to see her once, shortly after she had arrived. So she was quite surprised when one visiting day she was told that she had a visitor. "Me?" she asked incredulously.

"Yes, you. Thirty minutes. Get going," the guard said sharply.

Marian was flustered - who could be coming to see her? She was escorted to the visiting room, took a seat at the long table and waited under the watchful eye of the guard. In a few minutes the door opened and an older gentleman was led to the table where she was sitting. He pulled out the chair and seated himself, nodding his thanks to the guard. It took only a few seconds for Marian to recognize him. She was face to face with the father of the man she had murdered. Oh, it was him all right. He looked tired and his hair was much grayer than she remembered, but it had been fifteen years since she last saw him. Staring at him, she willed her
~~~

heart to stop banging in her chest, and forced a smile.

~20~

"Marian," he said, reaching for her hand.

"I . . ." she didn't know what to say, much less what to call him. She barely knew this man, having seen him only a few times since her wedding. Mister? Doctor? Dad? No, not Dad.

Sensing her discomfort, he offered a suggestion. "Marian, call me Matthew," he told her softly.

"Hello, Matthew," she breathed, wondering what was coming next.

"First, I'd like to say I'm sorry about your mother," he said. "I realize my condolences are late in coming, but the circumstances . . . ."

"Thank you," she whispered.

"I'm sure you're wondering why I'm here," he began. She nodded.

"I've learned that you'll be eligible for parole in five years, and I want you to know that I . . ."

She held up her hand to stop him. "I understand fully. I deserve nothing," she said.

"Marian, listen to me," he said. "I'm going to put in a good word for you."

"What?" she said, shocked by what he said.

"After Robert's . . . ah, death, his mother and I had to go through all of his things, as there was no one else. We learned a lot about him that we hadn't known before," he said, shaking his head. Marian began to cry. She wanted to tell this man how sorry she was for what she had done, but how could she? Whatever could she say that would help relieve the pain of losing his only son?

"I'm so sorry, Matthew. I'm just so terribly sorry."

He reached in his pocket, pulled out a clean white handkerchief, and handed it to her. The guard was there in a flash to see what he was giving her. She had the cloth opened and inspected before Marian could even reach for it. Even though visitors had to pass through an inspection before entering this room, occasionally things still slipped through. When she was assured that it was, in fact, just a handkerchief, she handed it to Marian with a look of warning. Marian took it and pressed it to her eyes.

"I don't expect you to forgive me," she continued, "but I'm really so ashamed and sorry."

"Marian, I have to be honest with you. A part of me still hates you for what you did, but I've learned a lot about Robert. He wasn't the man we thought he was. I couldn't talk about it until now because of his mother; she wouldn't allow it, but since her death I feel that I should," he told her.

"Her death?" Marian asked.

"Yes, she died eight months ago. I'm all alone now and I wanted to talk to you."

"I'm sorry for your loss," she said quietly.

Time was running out - he had to talk fast.

"I learned some pretty awful things about my son;

not only how he treated you, but other things as well. I blame myself to a point," he said, and continued to tell her how Robert had gotten himself into a jam at the hospital one time and Matthew had used his clout to get his son out of trouble. It was wrong, and he often wondered what the family of the patient would think of him if they knew. The patient survived, but suffered much, including another operation. It seemed after that, Robert thought of himself as invincible and so did everyone else. He chose not to mention to Marian evidence he had found, linking his son to other women while he was married to her.

"I saw him as a rising star; my rising star I guess, and I wanted him to have the best. I paid for everything. I think now that I made it much too easy for him."

"Time's up!" the guard yelled.

Matthew pushed back his chair and stood. Marian did the same and handed him his handkerchief.

"I won't be coming back this way again, Marian, I'm sorry to say. I'm going home now and put my house on the market to sell. I don't need all that space - never did really, but Mildred loved it. I've retired from my practice - maybe I'll play a little golf. I want you to know that I have forgiven you and I'm sorry for all you've been through," he told her soberly. "I regret many things."

"So do I, Matthew - so do I." She wanted to ask him to write to her occasionally, but then thought better of it and didn't. "Thank you so much for coming." Marian thought that thirty minutes had never passed so quickly in all the time she had been in prison. She was led back to her cell where Stella was waiting to hear about the visitor.

"Stella, I can't talk right now, okay? I promise I'll tell you everything in a bit, but now I need to lie down," she said.

"Fine with me," Stella told her, with some impatience in her voice.

Marian lay down on her bunk and curled up on her side with her back to her cell-mate. Tears were flowing and she couldn't stop them. He had forgiven her. Robert's father had said, "I want you to know that I've forgiven you . . ." and he had come all this way to tell her. For the first time in many years she felt relief. Maybe she would get out of here and be able to do something with her life after all. Maybe she had a chance - just maybe.

~~~

Four years and eight months after Matthew's visit, Marian was told that parole was being considered for her and she would appear before the board the following day. Sleep didn't come easy for her that night, and she was relieved when the six o'clock wake-up bell sounded the next morning. It seemed that her cell-mate was more excited than Marian was herself.

"I know you'll get paroled. I just know it," Stella told her over and over again. "You've been a perfect inmate. I know that better than anyone."

"Thank you, Stella, but I just don't know. . . ."

~~~

Marian sat on a wooden chair before the parole board with her hands folded in her lap. She had no expectations whatsoever; this mentality prevented disappointment. She stared at her hands, her brain processing only bits and pieces of what was being said.

" . . . your father-in-law . . . the crime was heinous . . . no prior criminal activity . . . time already served . . . a model prisoner. We, the board, have voted unanimously in favor of your parole." She never raised her eyes; had she heard correctly?

"You must stay in this state and report to your parole officer every three months for one year; after that you are free to go and do what you please. I wish you well, Marian."

She was stunned - she was finished here. She rose from her chair and managed to say, "Thank you very much," before she started to cry. The guard led her back to her cell where Stella was waiting to hear the news. They hugged each other, while they laughed and cried, and danced around the cell.

"I wish you could come with me," Marian told her friend.

"Not as much as I do, I bet!" Stella replied.

Marian had spent very little of the money she had earned working in the prison laundry and library. It had accumulated over the years and would be given to her on her last day, along with the few things she had with her when she entered prison.

~21~

A new beginning - that's how Marian saw her life now. She had taken back her maiden name and was going to make the best of what life she had left. She still regretted and couldn't justify what she had done, but Robert's father had forgiven her and she had done time.

Again, she had gotten on a bus, ridden to a new town and settled in. She remained in the state as ordered. Never could she remember having so little money, but somehow she felt rich. She was free. She found a furnished studio apartment in the heart of this town and worked as a waitress at The Best Family Restaurant down the street. They loved her at Best's, as it was known, because she would work weekends and was eager to fill in if someone called in sick. What else did she have to do? She loved the work and the customers. The restaurant was open Monday thru Saturday until 9:00 p.m. and closed at 6:00 p.m. on Sundays. She always arrived home before ten in the evening. Every time she let herself into the apartment and locked the door, she smiled. *She* was locking the door from the inside to keep anyone outside from coming into her home. It would take some time for her to get used to that concept. Inside her home, she could do what she pleased. Soaking in the bathtub was a favorite thing to do. The privacy was overwhelming to her. The only privacy she'd had for almost fifteen years was inside of her head. Sleeping was blissful too. There was no guard walking past the door randomly all through the night; and no sounds of women crying softly into their pillows, or snoring as they slept flat on their backs. It was, indeed, wonderful.

Having very little money, she was doing without a car. She loved the freedom of walking and most things were close to her home. She walked the four blocks to work each day, and became acquainted with most of the shops along the way. One of her favorites was a small florist/gift shop called Iris. It was in an old building that looked as if it had been a grocery store at one time. A single stained-glass iris, framed in clear leaded glass, hung from two silver cords in the large window beside the entrance. Over the door a wooden sign read simply, IRIS. The shop always intrigued her as she passed by; and one day she noticed a sign in the window that read: Special - Tulips - $4.00 a bunch. This she could not resist, and stopped in on her way home from work. Picking a bunch of yellow tulips from the pail on the floor, she browsed through the store.

"I can take those up to the counter if you'd like," a young girl said.

"Thank you. I'd like to look around. This is a lovely shop," she told the girl.

"Take your time and if you have any questions,

I'll be in back."

The girl was arranging fresh flowers in the back room and could watch the front of the store through a window; she seemed to be the only one working. Marian took her time. How long had it been since she had done something this simple? She was so happy - life was good. She spotted a small porcelain figurine of a white cat on one of the display shelves. Carefully she picked it up and turned it over to see the price. It was very nicely made, and she was surprised to see how inexpensive it was. She would buy this too; flowers and a knick-knack for her home. *Home*, how she loved the sound of that word! She placed the cat on the counter beside the flowers.

"Are you all set then?" the girl asked, as she came out from the back.

"Yes. I think this will be all for today."

"Oh, that's a cute figurine you've chosen. They're ten percent off today," she told her. Marian hadn't noticed the sign above the shelf.

"Well, that's great. I've been admiring that iris hanging in the window. It's absolutely beautiful," she said, as the girl rang up her purchases.

"Oh, that's not for sale though. It was specially made for the owner's wife. The shop was named for her," she explained, taking Marian's money from her.

Marian smiled, knowing if it was for sale, she couldn't afford it; but she could look at it every day as she passed on her way to work. The girl told her, at times during the year, when the sun is at a certain angle and shines on the frame, it casts rainbows all around the store.

"It's really very pretty," she added. "I'll wrap these tulips up for you and here's your change." She disappeared into the back somewhere for a minute and returned with the tulips wrapped in clear cellophane, tied with a narrow yellow ribbon.

"Goodness, the wrapping is as pretty as the flowers," Marian exclaimed.

"That's the way the boss likes it. Is the cat a gift? I'll wrap that too, if you'd like."

"No, it's for me; I had a cat once . . . a long time ago." The girl rolled the figurine in tissue paper and placed it in a small paper bag that was decorated with irises.

Marian smiled as she walked home with her treasures. Yellow tulips were her favorites. She found a drinking glass in the kitchen cupboard and filled it with water from the tap. The arrangement looked nice on the table by the window. She made a mental note to pick up an inexpensive vase when she was out; at these prices, she could always have it filled with fresh flowers.

Her new home was one room - a studio apartment with a studio couch. There was a small kitchenette and a bathroom. What more did she need? It came furnished, but she had to buy towels and sheets. Dishes, cutlery and a few odd pots and pans were in the cupboards. Not much else was needed. A few towels, one set of sheets, some dish towels and she was set. She did buy new glasses, since the ones on the shelf were limed up from the dishwasher. Not sure if she had ever been inside a Wal-Mart store before, she was getting very familiar with it now and was grateful to Sam Walton. They even had clothes there. Smiling, she would look through the racks and remember back when she wore nothing but designer things. Strangely, she was more content now. Uniforms were worn at the restaurant, so she really didn't need much. She noticed how the styles had changed while she was away too. It was almost as if she had been reborn - everything was new again. She'd had her hair cut and styled shortly after arriving, so she felt that she looked up-to-date even though she felt years behind.

The cat figurine was placed on the table next to the couch. Looking at it once more before she turned out the light that night; she knew that she would like to get another cat someday. Mabelina was probably dead by now. Marian hoped she'd had a good life.

~~~

There were two important phone calls that Marian wanted to make, and she planned to do it today. She had worked the early shift, so she had time this afternoon. The phone was answered on the second ring.

"Walker Day-Care, Kristen speaking." It had a new name.

"I wonder if you could help me? A woman named Flora Hickman once worked at your day-care. It's been a long time now, but would you happen to know her?" Marian asked.

"No, Ma'am, I don't. The day-care changed hands ten years ago and the new owners brought in all of their own people. No one has been here longer than that. I'm sorry I can't help more."
~~~

"Oh, that's all right. Thank you for your time. Good-bye."

Next, she called information.

"I have a listing for a Donald Hickman, a Dr. James Hickman, and a William Hickman," the woman on the phone said.

James could be Flora's son. Marian asked for that number and thanked the woman. Would it be possible to talk to her old friend one more time? Dialing the number, she hoped that she could.

"Dr. Hickman's residence," a woman said.

"Hello. I'm not sure I have the right number, but maybe you can help me. I'm trying to locate Flora Hickman. Would she be a relative of yours?" Marian asked.

"I'm Lorraine, her daughter-in-law. Who is this?"

"My name is Marian and I worked with Flora at the day-care over fifteen years ago. We became good friends and I would like to get in touch with her, if possible. I've been away for a long time," she explained.

"I'm sorry to tell you that Flora passed on three years ago," Lorraine said sadly.

"Oh, I'm so sorry to hear that. She meant a lot to me and I was hoping to talk with her. Was she ill?" Marian asked.

"No, actually it was quite unexpected. She died peacefully in her sleep."

"Your husband was in medical school when we worked together. Flora was so proud," Marian said, remembering how her friend had talked at length about her son.

"Yes, my husband is a surgeon."

"Well, I really hoped the news would be better, but it's been nice talking to you, Lorraine, and thank you for your time. Good-bye."

"Good-bye, Marian."

Marian was disappointed. She wanted to talk to Flora and catch up on the past fifteen years, but it wasn't to be. "Rest in peace, old friend," she whispered.

~22~

The first year passed quickly for Marian. Faithfully, every three months she had checked in with her parole officer; and now she could go wherever she wished, but she felt very much at home where she was. She considered looking for a larger place, but made the decision to stay and renewed her lease on the apartment. Everything was so conveniently located for her that she still hadn't bought a car. If she moved, she may need one. She had a few friends at work and knew the neighborhood well - why should she move? Also, she had learned that pets were allowed in this building; another good reason to stay put.

She had become a regular at the grocery store close to her apartment and, of course, at the Iris flower shop. At least once a week she bought fresh flowers and put them in the vase she found at Wal-Mart. The owner, Philip Youngberg, was a widower. He and his wife had worked together for twenty-two years in the store, and it had been his idea to name the store for her. He missed her a lot and never could find a replacement who worked as well as she had.

~~~

Philip's wife had been dead for more than five years, but he had never found another woman who interested him; until now that is. This woman named Marian who came in every week did indeed pique his interest, but she showed no sign of interest in him. It had been a long time since he had asked someone for a date and wasn't comfortable even thinking about it. One Saturday afternoon, when she was in the store to buy yellow tulips, they struck up a conversation that was more personal than the usual, "How are you today? Nice weather . . . ," that they usually had.

"So, yellow tulips must be your favorite, right?" he began hesitantly.

"Yes, they are," she said laughing. She looked so pretty when she laughed.

"Maybe I should get some of these daisies for a change," she murmured.

"Tell you what," he said. "I'll arrange some daisies in a vase for you as a gift. You are my most regular customer, you know."

"Oh, you don't have to do that. I'll just buy a bunch," she told him, and then noticed the way he was looking at her. He wanted to do this for her.

"That would be very nice, Philip. Thank you." He was one of the nicest men she had ever met. He wasn't a "Golden Boy" or anything close. He was just a man - a very kind man. He was attractive, well-groomed, and she had thought about him more than once in the past year, but knew there was no chance for her with him. She walked around the
~~~

shop while he made up the arrangement in the back. She felt him watching her and tried to act as though she didn't. Marian - *stop it*, she told herself silently.

"Well, how do these look?" he asked, returning to the front of the store. " I can do something different, if you'd like," he said, wanting to please her.

"They're beautiful! I've never seen daisies look so pretty," she exclaimed. He really had fussed.

"Do you think you can carry them home though?" he asked. "I could have them delivered for you." He had never seen her drive and knew she lived somewhere close by.

"I think I can manage them," she said. After all, they were a gift; she didn't expect more.

"I have an idea," he started, not knowing where he had gotten the nerve. "I could bring them over myself, and maybe we could go have a cup of coffee. Do you drink coffee? That coffeehouse across the street has the best . . ." He was jabbering like a schoolboy. "I'm sorry," he said. "Maybe I'm out of line here."

"No, not at all," she told him. "I think that would be nice, especially after these beautiful flowers, but I'd insist on buying the coffee."

He couldn't believe how easy it had been. Why had he waited so long?

"It's almost five o'clock," he said, glancing at the clock on the wall. "Maybe it's too late for coffee. Would some supper be better? I know a great place at the edge of town . . . they have great food . . ." He was jabbering again and watching her closely.

"Oh, I don't know, Philip," she said softly, then wondered what the harm would be. Supper with a nice man - what could it hurt? And how often did she have a Saturday off from work? "Well, maybe I could," she told him. "What time?"

"I usually close the shop at six on Saturday. I could bring your flowers to you then, if it's okay," he told her.

"That would be fine. Is this place casual?" she asked.

"Oh yes, very. You look fine just the way you are," he said, thinking that she would look good in a gunny sack.

"Okay," she said, smiling at him. "I'll see you then." She told him where she lived and that he could park his car in the lot behind the apartment building. He handed her the tulips wrapped in cellophane and yellow ribbon and felt her hand touch his for just a second.

"Marian!" he called, as she went out the door. "I forgot to give you your change." Boy, was he rattled or what? She stopped and took the money from him and gave him another one of her smiles. Damn, he thought she was pretty.

Marian nearly ran home. She hadn't even made up the studio couch that morning; often she didn't on weekends. Excitedly, she unlocked the door and dropped her purse and tulips on the counter. He would be here in less than one hour. She made up the couch and looked around the small room. Everything else was in order. She washed her face, reapplied what little makeup she wore, and brushed her hair. Should she change her clothes? He said she looked okay. Maybe just the blouse - yes, she would just change her blouse.

When Philip arrived, she was ready. Even the tulips had been placed in the vase by the window.

She opened the door and felt something flutter in her stomach. Wasn't she too old for that sort of thing? He looked so nice, standing there with the daisies in his hand, she just stared at him for a minute.

"Aren't you going to let me come in?" he asked.

She laughed and stepped aside so he could enter her home. He was the first visitor she had ever had here. "I'm sorry. I'm not very used to having company," she told him.

They had a nice time together that evening. After supper, they had coffee at the coffeehouse across from his shop. He learned that she was a widow and had no children, but she'd offered no more about herself. What had she done since then and why had she moved to this town, he wondered, but didn't ask. He was just so happy that she had. He had parked his car at the Iris and they walked across the street for coffee. When it was time to take her home, they walked together slowly to her building.

"Thank you so much for tonight, Philip. I had a wonderful time," she told him, sincerely, when they got to her door.

"I thank you for going with me," he said. "I'm sure I'll see you . . . let me think, tulips are good for about five days, right? That would be Thursday." He wished he could put his arms around her and hug her, but didn't. There was something elusive about this woman - he wouldn't rush her in any way.

After Philip left, Marian closed her apartment door and leaned against it. Why hadn't she met him twenty-five years ago instead of . . . she didn't even like to say his name. Should she have asked Philip to come in? No, that would be too bold she thought, and they'd already had coffee. No, tonight was perfect.

~23~

Marian was awake long after she went to bed Saturday night, going over all the things she had learned about Philip. He was sixty-one years old, had two sons and a granddaughter named Katie, who was three. One son lived close by and one lived in another state; unfortunately, the son with the daughter was the one who lived far away. Philip said they kept in touch by phone and visited when they could, but he missed the little girl. Never having had a daughter, he thought she was amazing.

Philip lay awake as well that Saturday night, realizing how little he had learned about Marian. Had he talked too much? No, he had asked her many times to tell him about herself. Maybe she's just shy, he thought and rolled over one more time in an effort to find a comfortable position in bed. He hoped he wouldn't have to wait until Thursday to see her again.

All day Sunday, both Philip and Marian thought of each other, but neither made a phone call. When Monday morning came, he was working in his shop and found himself watching the front window, hoping to see her walk by on her way to work. He wasn't sure what shift she was working that day and thought he had missed her when she surprised him and came into the shop a little after six o'clock that evening.

"Hello, Philip," she said. "I just wanted to stop by and thank you again for Saturday night. I really enjoyed it."

"So did I," he said. "Maybe we can do it again sometime."

"That would be nice. I could use a friend," she told him.

Friend? he thought. He was hoping for more than that, but said, "I guess you don't close tonight."

"No, I went in at ten this morning. I like this shift really," she told him.

"Isn't it hard though, working different hours every day?" he asked, trying to keep the conversation going so she would stay.

"No, not really. I'm alone so it doesn't matter," she said, gazing around the shop to see if he had gotten any new merchandise. "Well, I sure don't need flowers yet, so I guess I'll be going."

Oh, don't go, he thought. "Would you like to go out Saturday night?" he asked hopefully.

"Oh, thanks Philip, but I work until nine that night," she told him.

"Well, how about another night. You name it." He really wanted to get to know her. She just seemed so right and he'd been alone a long time.

She wanted to say, tonight, right now, but didn't. How could she do this? She couldn't lead him on and then tell him to go away, and she certainly couldn't tell him about her past. "I get off work at three tomorrow; I'll stop in then and we can decide, okay?"

"Great. I'll be here," he told her.

"I'll see you then," she said, and waved as she left the store. Slowly she walked home wondering what in the world to do about Philip. Maybe she could just keep her past a secret and go with her feelings. No. She knew that she could fall for this guy; she also knew that it wouldn't be right to get serious and have a secret from him. What was she going to do? Oh, stop it, she told herself, you've gone out with him one time - grow up. But he was so nice; he seemed *right.* She *had* been out with him only one time, but she had thought about him a lot. She knew that she could love this man, she had watched him from afar for a year, and now she had spent time alone with him too. Yes, she could love this man. Never would she have started anything herself; he started all of this. What could she do?

The following day she stopped at the Iris after work as she said she would. Philip had a new employee working with him. The young girl who had worked for him had quit to go away to college.

"Hi, Marian," Philip called from the back room when she entered the shop.

The new employee politely asked if Marian needed some help.

"No, thank you. I stopped in to see Philip," she told her. He came up to the front of the store and introduced the two women.

"Jenna, I'd like you to meet Marian, she's a very

regular customer, you'll get to know her well," he said. "Marian, this is Jenna." The women smiled and shook hands.

"It's nice to meet you, Jenna," Marian said.

"Nice to meet you too, and now if you'll excuse me," Jenna said and went to the back room to busy herself with the fresh flowers.

Philip and Marian stood together looking out the window of the shop.

"What did you decide?" he asked her.

Not sure when she had made up her mind, she told him, "I think Friday would be okay for me. Would that be good for you? I'll be off work around three."

"Friday would be fine," he said, wishing it was Thursday today instead of Tuesday.

"So how's the new girl working out?" Marian asked. She wasn't really a girl, she looked to Marian to be somewhere in her forties.

"She seems to be doing well," he told her. "I'm hoping to be able to take a little more time off now that she's here. She's been in the floral business for years, so she knows what she's doing. I hope she'll be able to keep Todd in line too." Todd was the part-time delivery boy and he needed watching. He was a good worker if someone kept an eye on him.

Marian walked home with a troubled mind. She had no idea what to do about this very nice man who had a definite interest in her. She would stay away from the shop for the next few days and see him on Friday.

~~~
~~~

He rang her doorbell at exactly five o'clock on Friday. When she opened the door, she burst out laughing. His face was completely hidden by a huge arrangement of yellow tulips.

"Well, I missed you yesterday; I thought you'd come in to buy fresh ones and when you didn't, I figured I'd bring you some," he told her, laughing now too.

"Some? Philip! How many are there?" It was the biggest bouquet of tulips she had ever seen, and they were beautiful. "Oh, thank you. They're so pretty," she said, touching his arm just before she took the flowers from him. It didn't go unnoticed by him. She placed the tulips on the kitchen counter as it was the only surface large enough to hold the massive array.

"Where would you like to go?" he asked. "We could try something different."

"I really liked the place we went to last week, but if you have something else in mind. . . ."

"Well, I do know of a few places around here. My wife loved going out for dinner. She never wanted to cook after she had been on her feet all day in the shop," he told her.

"I don't blame her," Marian said, wondering what his wife had been like. She envied the dead woman and felt silly for it.

Philip chose the restaurant - not the same one as last time. They were all new to Marian, who hadn't eaten anywhere but the place she worked, and her own home. She loved the fact that she could buy and cook *whatever* she wanted. It sure beat going through a cafeteria line with a plastic tray.

Someday, she would cook for Philip, she thought. He was probably tired of eating out and would love a home cooked meal.

This restaurant was a bit fancier than the last, and darker. It was very romantic. He took her hand in his while they were waiting for dessert, and she loved the feel of his big hand over hers. What was she going to do?

"Thank you for coming with me, Marian. I like being with you very much," he told her.

"I do too, Philip. I really do," she said quietly.

~24~

It went on like this for three months. Philip was frustrated and even confided his confusion to Jenna.

"What do you suppose I'm doing wrong, Jenna?" he asked one day as they worked side by side in the back.

"What makes you think it's you. Maybe it's her," she replied. "I have seen the way she looks at you though, Philip. Her feelings are pretty obvious."

"So what's the problem then? She's holding back something, I know. Not that I expected her to throw off her clothes the first night . . . I would like to hold her more and talk about what *could* be, but she avoids all that. She thinks of me as a friend." He shook his head and went to the cooler for more flowers for the arrangement he was making. "She couldn't be a lesbian could she, Jenna?" he asked over his shoulder. "No, she doesn't even look like one," he said, answering his own question.

Jenna smiled, her boss thought that all lesbians looked the same with short hair and masculine ways, but she said nothing. She had gotten to know Philip well since starting to work for him; he trusted her.

She'd even had him over for dinner, and her husband liked him too.

"Maybe you should just sit down and have a talk. Tell her how you feel. That's the only way you'll find out," she told him.

"That wouldn't upset her?" he wondered.

"I don't know, but you're upset, aren't you? I don't think you'd be out of line, Philip. You just want to know if you're wasting your time, right?" Jenna said.

"Right," he said, and made up his mind to do just what Jenna suggested. He would have a talk with Marian, soon.

The next time Marian came in for yellow tulips, Jenna talked to her a bit and then slipped into the back, so Philip and Marian could talk privately.

"Do we have a date this week?" he asked. It was sort of a habit for them now. Once or twice a week they would have supper together, or go see a movie, but that was all. Philip had finally managed to kiss her good-bye every time they parted, and could tell that she was eager for more, but it never happened.

"I thought I'd cook for you this week," she told him. "If that's all right with you. I'm not a bad cook, if I say so myself." She was smiling at him.

"That would be great. I'm a rotten cook so maybe you can give me some hints," he said. They made plans for Friday that week. She would cook beef Wellington and he would bring the wine. This, he thought, is perfect. We can talk about things in the privacy of her home much better than in a restaurant.

Marian had made this special meal a few times for doctor friends and their wives. It had always been a big hit, but that was a very long time ago. She bought a cookbook at Wal-Mart the next day, as she couldn't remember just how to prepare it, and wanted it to be perfect for Philip. She read the recipe over twice and made a list of the things she would need from the grocery store. There was a butcher shop as well as a packaged meat counter in the grocery where she shopped; she would buy a choice piece of tenderloin. She would need pate and ingredients for the Bordelaise Sauce too. Not having cooked anything this special in a long time, she was excited and happy to be doing it for such a nice man.

~~~

At three o'clock on Friday, Marian was ready to leave the restaurant. Usually she stayed a few minutes after, as there had been no hurry, but today was different. The other waitresses noticed that today Marian seemed different somehow.

"So, what's up ?" one of them asked her. "Got a hot date? You sure are in a hurry to get out of here today." Marian laughed and shrugged it off.

"I've got something to do that I've been putting off, that's all," she told her.

"Yeah, right," the woman said.

Philip was coming at five o'clock. She would roast the beef for thirty minutes, cool it in the fridge, and prepare the pastry that would cover the roast. That would bake for forty-five minutes or until brown. Maybe they should eat later, she thought; there was so much to do. Her head was spinning - maybe she should have made a meat loaf. "No, no, this will be fine," she told herself. They had all evening, and
~~~

she had a feeling that something would happen tonight, but she wasn't sure just what.

She had finished everything with fifteen minutes to spare. The roast was ready to put back in the oven, the salad was made, the Bordelaise Sauce was started and would be finished later when the meat was done. The table was set with matching place mats and napkins, a candle burned in the center. Everything looked nice.

She sat down on the couch and waited for him. She had no right to feel this excited, did she? Maybe she would forget the past, just for tonight, and enjoy this wonderful man. Before she could decide, the bell rang and she felt her heart quicken.

"Philip," she breathed when she saw him. "Come in." He was juggling two bottles of wine and a small arrangement of violets he had made up specially for her.

"Here, let me help you," she said, reaching for something. He didn't know what to let go of for fear of dropping something.

"Let me set this on the counter," he said and put the violets down. Then he could maneuver the wine bottles better. "I brought two reds - didn't know which would be best."

"Oh, either of these would be good, thanks. And these violets are so pretty, thank you," she said and put the flowers up to her nose to inhale their fragrance. "I think there's room on the table for these. You're so sweet, Philip."

"You're very welcome," he told her smiling.

"Shall we have a glass of wine first?" she asked. "The meat has to bake awhile."

They sat on the couch enjoying the wine and soon the mouth watering smell of the roasting beef filled the room.

"That sure smells good, Marian. What did you say you were making?" he asked.

"Beef Wellington. It's special - for you."

"Well, how do I rate?" he teased. "I can't remember if I've ever had that before. If I have, I've forgotten."

"I hope you like it," she said and drained her wine glass. "I have to finish the sauce; want more wine?"

"I'll have more with dinner," he said.

The meat thermometer registered 140 degrees, the meat was done. The sauce was thickening on the stove, the salads were on the table, and the water glasses were filled.

"It's ready, Philip," she said.

The pastry was puffed and golden brown and beneath this delectable layer, the filet of beef was cooked to perfection. She watched him chew and knew he liked it.

"This is great, Marian. I've haven't tasted anything this good in a long time," he said. "Maybe you should be cooking at Best's instead of waiting tables." She was glad that she had gone to all the trouble; it was worth it, just to see him enjoy it so much.

After dinner, he helped her clear the table and load the dishwasher. For a moment, she pretended they were a couple. She started the coffee and went to join him on the couch. "Be sure to take that other bottle of wine home," she told him.

"No, you keep it," he said, "I'll be back."

"You know what I've been thinking about?" She was pouring coffee for them at the counter.

"No, what?" he asked.

"I think I want to get a cat. I had one a long time ago and I really loved having a pet," she said, handing him a mug of coffee.

"What happened to it?" he wondered, hoping to get a glimpse of her past.

"Oh, I moved and I had to get rid of her," she said softly. "I think I'd like a kitten; they're so sweet."

"We always had a dog," he told her. "A toy poodle; we named him Alex, hoping that sounded masculine. He went to work with us every day - he was our watchdog, which was a joke. He loved everybody who came into the shop and napped most of the day in the front window." They talked a bit more about general things and then Philip took on a serious look and the conversation changed. Hesitantly he asked her if there was anything she'd like to talk about - if something was wrong.

"What do you mean, is something wrong? Do you mean something wrong with me?" she asked.

"Well, I don't mean *wrong* exactly," he said. He was afraid he would blow this and never see her again, but he continued. "Marian I think a lot of you - truth is, I think I'm in love with you. I think you care for me too. I can feel it, but you have a . . . oh, I don't know. It seems like you have a shield of some kind around you and I can't get close to you. What is it?" She dropped her head and stared at the empty coffee mug in her hand. He took it from her and put his arm around her. "Can we talk about it?" he asked.

When she looked up, he could see tears in her eyes.

"What is it, Marian? What's wrong?"

"You don't know me, Philip. You don't know anything about me," she said.

"That's the point! I don't know anything about you, but I want to. I can't go on like this much longer; I want to know you," he told her.

"No, you don't, Philip. You really don't."

"Please. You can tell me anything. I can't keep hoping that someday we'll be together if that can't happen. I feel like we're playing a game and I hate it," he said.

She had known that eventually it would come to this.

~25~

They talked far into Saturday morning. She told him everything and he promised to keep her secret to himself, no matter what happened between the two of them. She had taken a huge risk - but she had done that before.

Philip was stunned by what she told him, and lay awake all night, tossing in his bed until he finally gave up any hope for sleep and went to the shop at six in the morning. He felt like hell, but they were doing a wedding at eleven o'clock and he couldn't leave Jenna alone with that.

Marian didn't sleep either. She felt relieved in a way - she had unburdened herself, but she would miss him so . . . it was over, she was sure of that. Philip said he would have to think about what she told him. He needed time and he didn't know how much. She told him that she would move out of the neighborhood and he wouldn't ever have to see her again; she would understand.

The unopened bottle of wine sat on the counter as a reminder of what had been, and for the first time in a very long time, no yellow tulips graced the spot on the table by the window. Her life was gray; she rode a bus the few short blocks to work, or walked a different way to avoid the Iris.

Philip was distant at work and Jenna could stand it no longer.

"Philip, tell me what's wrong. We can't work like this - we barely speak to each other," she said.

"Oh, Jenna, I wish I could talk to someone about this, but believe me, I can't," he told her.

"Well, I know it has something to do with Marian. She never comes in anymore. Did she move away?"

"No, but she might," he said.

"Well, go with her! What's wrong with you, Philip? You two are so good together. I don't get it," she said and stomped off into the back room.

That's what he had thought, they were so good together . . . . He could think of little else over the next few weeks. He missed her, but wasn't sure what he would do. He had hoped to get to know her and ask her to marry him. He missed having a wife, but how the hell could he sleep in the same bed with her? How could he be sure he would wake up the next morning? Oh, don't be stupid, he would think. She paid for what she did, and her father-in-law had even forgiven her. Back and forth, every day, this argument went on inside his head. It had been three weeks and two days since that fateful Friday night. That's how he thought of that night - fateful Friday. But what if she hadn't told him and gotten involved with him; he thought that would be worse, so he gave her credit for that. Never in his life had he been up against something like this.

He would lie in bed at night for hours, weighing this predicament in his mind. The guy was a jerk, that was a given. Even jerks don't deserve to be murdered. Why did she marry a man she didn't know? Well, what the hell good did it do to wonder about that? Hindsight. She'd never even had a parking ticket before that. Doesn't matter, it was murder! She had turned herself in too, that was good. He had a list of pros and cons in his head and it seemed to him, that after much pondering, the list of pros was much longer. But did he dare get involved - Jesus - he didn't know what to do. What he did know though, was that he loved her.

It had been nearly four weeks since Marian told Philip the truth. She said she would wait for his answer no matter how long it took him, but now she was anxious. What if he didn't have the nerve to face her? She wouldn't blame him for any reaction he might have. At times she felt like she did deserve some happiness, but then would remind herself that it was *murder*, not armed robbery or some lesser charge. But she was so different now. She wanted to tell Philip - she wasn't that person anymore. She remembered the huge cricket she had found under the sink and how she caught it in a paper cup and let it out the window. And the little kids at the day-care where she worked, she couldn't have harmed them any more than she could fly. She regretted so much what she had done, even to this day. She had served time in prison, but felt now that she would pay for her crime the rest of her life. She would never figure out how she actually had planned and committed that act. Never.

Blinded by rage?

She hadn't heard from Philip yet and it had been four weeks. Both their lives were in limbo.

~~~

Marian came home from work with a carry-out meal in a bag for her dinner. She set it on the counter and went into the bathroom to wash her hands when the phone rang.

"Hello," she said.

"Marian," he said softly.

"Oh, Philip . . . ," she could hardly speak.

"I need to see you, Marian. Is this a good time?"

"Yes, it's fine."

"I'll be there in ten minutes," he said and hung up. He sounded so serious, it frightened her. She quickly washed her hands, changed her clothes, and ran a brush through her hair. Then the doorbell rang. She couldn't believe how nervous she was. What would he have to say? She opened the door. He looked tired, but managed a smile for her. He had a bunch of yellow tulips in his hand.

"These are for you," he said. She took the flowers and turned to put them on the counter. He came up behind her and put his arms around her. He kissed the top of her head. "I love you, Marian," he whispered into her hair. She turned to face him and started to say something, but his mouth covered hers and she couldn't.

"I missed you so much!" she told him when she could speak. She was crying now and wouldn't let go of him. They were locked in an embrace exactly where they stood for several minutes. "Does this mean that we can be together?" she asked sniffling.
~~~

"That's what I've wanted for a long time, you know."

"Well, you sure didn't act like you did," he told her.

"Philip, I couldn't! What if I had gotten involved and then told you, and you couldn't deal with it, what then? Can you deal with it?" she asked anxiously. "You haven't said yet."

"I've done nothing but think about it since that night," he told her honestly.

"And?" she was afraid to get her hopes up.

"I said I love you. I just may need to talk about it some more, if you don't mind," he said. He pulled her to him and kissed her again.

She didn't want him to leave - ever. "Don't go home tonight, Philip," she whispered.

They shared the carry-out meal from the restaurant, opened the bottle of wine that had been sitting on the counter since that night, and Philip didn't go home until morning.

~26~

Marian had never felt anything like this in all her life; this was love. She was walking on air, as they say, and wished she could be with Philip every minute. That, of course wasn't possible, but they were together as much as they could be. They talked for hours about her past; he asking questions, she answering as best she could. He was the only living soul who knew about her work at the day-care center. Only twice before had she told the whole story; once to the priest and then to Detective Dawson, all those years ago, but this was different.

One evening, after many hours spent in the past, Philip took her hands in his and said, "Marian, let's put the past to rest, okay? It's over."

"But Philip, I spent less than fifteen years in prison and he'll be dead forever," she lamented.

"That's true, what you did was despicable and you paid for it. You did exactly what the judge ordered. Wouldn't it be senseless to waste the rest of your life?"

"Yes, I suppose you're right," she said, hoping that she could leave her past behind and begin anew.

After supper they sat sipping coffee together at her kitchen table.

"I was wondering if you'd like to work with me at the shop?" he asked. "Jenna wants to go to part-time, so I'll need someone. Don't feel like you have to, but I wanted to ask you first."

Would she want to? She'd love to! "I don't know anything about flowers you know," she told him.

"You can learn," he said.

"I am getting a bit tired of waiting on tables," she said. "When do you need me?"

"As soon as possible. Jenna is eager to cut down, her daughter is having a baby soon and she wants to be free to help," he said.

"Jenna, a grandmother? She's so young!"

"So is her daughter - it's a long story," he told her.

Marian gave her notice at the restaurant and began working with Philip; she loved it. They worked side by side in the back room where she learned the art of flower arrangement. It came quite natural to her he thought, and he liked having her there. He had been devastated when Iris died - he missed her by his side each day and never thought that he would feel this way about another woman again; but here he was, working next to a woman he loved with all his heart.

He was day-dreaming, something he often did when working with flowers. He thought it had something to do with inhaling the wonderful fragrance of the freshly cut flowers - endorphins, or something - he thought he'd read that somewhere.

"Philip!" she said, for the second time.

"What?"

"Are you awake?" she asked laughing. "I've been talking to you."

"Oh, sorry, my mind wanders when I do this, I guess," he said.

"Well, I guess. How does this look?"

"It looks fine. You're good at that you know," he told her.

"Thanks, but I mean does this arrangement look all right in *this* container?" She wasn't sure, but loved to experiment.

"I think it looks great. I bet someone will come in this afternoon and pick that very one," he told her.

Just then, the little bell over the door jingled, signaling a customer had come in.

"I'll get that," he said, and went to the front of the store. He was back in a few minutes. "More tulips," he told her. "Those things sell like crazy."

"How can you sell them so cheap?" she asked. They were still $4.00 a bunch.

"Well, it's easy really," he said. "The more I buy from the grower, the lower the price is for me, and if I keep them at $4.00, more people buy them. I make the same as if I sold them for $8.00 and bought fewer, because less people would buy them. Make sense?"

"Yes, it does," she said.

"Most important though, is that the customer is happy," he told her. "That's what business is all about; my business anyway."

She liked this about him too, he was not a greedy man. He ran his small business well and treated his customers with respect. He had no interest in expanding and becoming a huge enterprise, he just wanted to make a decent living and do a good job.

~~~

As the months passed, Marian proved to be very proficient at her job and was an asset to Philip and the business. He took her with him on buying trips too. She was good at choosing merchandise that sold quickly. The gift shop part of the business had grown considerably since she started eight months before. It was in need of a woman's touch.

"I've been thinking about something, Marian," he said one evening over dinner. "Tell me what you think." She put down her fork and listened.

"I said you should put your past to rest and I think I should do the same," he told her. "I think I'm going to change the name of the shop."

"Are you sure, Philip?" she asked puzzled. "It's a beautiful name and that iris hanging in the window is so perfect. Do you really want to do that?"

"Yes, I really do. As for that iris, I think I'll sell it. I know someone who would buy it. He works at the bank, and he asks me almost every time I see him if I want to sell it; he collects stained-glass art. I never thought I'd part with it, but I want to now," he told her. "I think we should get married soon and change the name of the shop - put the past to rest, as I said."

"Is that a proposal, Philip?" she asked surprised.

"Well, I guess it is," he said. "I didn't do that very well, did I? Will you marry me, Marian? I don't have a ring for you just yet, but I'll get one soon." That was not what he had planned, but he
~~~

knew her so well and felt close to her now - it just slipped out.

It hadn't bothered her at all, and she smiled at him.

"Well?" he asked.

"Well, I may have to think about it . . . okay, yes!" she said laughing.

"When? Is this weekend too soon?" he wondered.

"Yes. I have a lot to do, you know," she told him.

"I want to sell my house too, and get something that you and I pick out together." She had been to his home many times, it was a very nice house, but it had been another woman's. She thought he was right about them choosing something together and appreciated his thoughtfulness.

"When is your lease up?" he asked.

"Soon," she told him, "I've been there long enough now so I can sign a new one for three months if I want."

"That's great. Do you have any ideas for a new name for the shop?" he asked.

"Not really," she said.

"What attracted you the first time? What made you want to come in?"

"The tulips, $4.00 a bunch," she told him, "but I also loved the iris in the window. It's so beautiful."

"How does the Tulip Shack sound to you?" he asked, ignoring her comment about the iris. He had made his mind up about that, he wanted a change.

"Shack? Does that sound good?" she wondered. "Sounds like something run-down to me. Maybe Tulip Hut - is that better?"

"Let me think about it for a bit. We could put all the tulips in the front window . . . we'd have to rearrange some things too," he said, full of ideas now. "I want you to meet Phil and Margaret, and of course, Katie too. I've told them all about you and they seem happy for me and eager to know you." Marian had met Lance, Philip's younger son and they saw him quite often. She looked forward to meeting his older son and his family too.

"We'll have to look for a place to live . . . we *do* have a lot to do," he said seriously.

She simply smiled at him - unable to believe her good fortune; and so, the planning began.

~27~

Philip gave Marian a solitaire diamond set in yellow gold. It was stunning in its simplicity. A narrow gold band would complete the set when they married. It was worth many thousands of dollars less than her first engagement ring, but it meant so much more. She knew it was given in love.

Philip's house was on the market and Marian had signed a short term lease on the studio apartment she had called home for two years. They began shopping for a new home together. Every Sunday they read the real-estate section in the paper over morning coffee and planned their day around the open houses they wanted to see. They would be married in a small chapel near the shop in two months. Philip's son and his family would come for the wedding and after that a reception would be held for the family and friends. Maybe a short trip would follow, but none of this really mattered to the couple, they were just so happy to be together.

They found a condo that they liked a mile or so from the shop. It was a new construction, so they were able to pick out colors and carpet. Never had

Marian had such fun. She could choose what she wanted and it seemed that Philip always agreed with her choice. They had very similar taste when it came to decorating and that made it easy. They shopped for furniture, curtains, dishes, sheets, towels, and everything else they would need to make this their home. They would keep some of Philip's furnishings too. He had a beautiful bedroom set that Marian wanted to keep for the guest room in the condo, but they would buy a new set for themselves. They were both beginning anew.

"Are you sure you want to sell that iris, Philip?" Marian asked. They were rearranging things in the shop. The iris had been taken down and set on the floor against the wall in the back room.

"Yes, I'm sure. I need to wrap it up so it's ready to go," he said.

"I can do that for you," she told him. It was so beautiful she didn't know how he could part with it, but the man from the bank had offered a very nice price, and Philip had agreed. The deal was done.

The shop was beginning to take on a whole new look. The shelves were moved and more were added at Marian's request. She had taken charge of the gift shop and the merchandise there. She had a way of arranging things so they were very appealing to the eye, and it was successful. Not only did people come in regularly to buy tulips, they also spent more time browsing in the gift section. Life was good and at times Marian completely forgot what brought her to this part of the country. They both agreed that her past would be kept between the two of them.

She had paid for what she did, but they felt it was a part of her that belonged to them only and they talked about it less and less as time passed.

The shop was renamed. It was now the Tulip Hut and the window seat was filled with tulips of all colors and various arrangements. This was Marian's job too, and each morning she made sure the flowers looked nice, replacing those that were wilted with fresh ones from the cooler in back of the store. It was quite stunning and often people would stop just to gaze at the array of tulips, but mostly they came in and bought a bunch or two. The sign was new, but the price remained the same. TULIPS $4.00 a bunch. A wooden sign over the door read: TULIP HUT, replacing IRIS. Everything had changed and they were so happy. The customers were as well. At first, many of them thought the shop had changed hands and were happy to learn that it had not. They congratulated the couple on their engagement and complimented them on the changes they had made.

~~~

The wedding day was rapidly approaching and the condo was completely finished. The new furniture would be delivered in a few days. Philip had sold his house and had most of the furniture moved out; what they were keeping was in the condo and other things were given away. They had worked hard these past weeks and managed to keep the shop going as well. Jenna helped as much as she could too. She worked full time for three weeks to help them out and they appreciated it greatly. She had even taken time to help Marian pick out a wed-
~~~

ding outfit and she and her husband were going to stand up for the couple at the ceremony.

Marian, with Jenna's help, chose a two piece pale blue silk dress; she hadn't worn anything so fine in many years, but this was special. The skirt was long and the jacket was short, it was simple and beautiful. She would carry a small bouquet of flowers made specially for her by Jenna.

Philip's son and his family would arrive two days before the wedding and stay for three days after that. The new couple planned to go to a bed and breakfast for their wedding night, but would be back home sometime the next day. They wanted to spend as much time with Philip's family as possible, they could plan a honeymoon trip anytime.

Philip now lived in the condo, but Marian would stay in the studio apartment until they were married. She felt that she should, and she had nothing to move but her clothes and personal items, so that made it easy. She spent a lot of time at the condo however, and loved being there. It was beautiful - bright and sunny, with a southern exposure and a skylight in the kitchen and bathroom. There would be no gloomy days living here.

~~~

Marian was practicing her driving skills as much as she could, she would need a car after they were married; she wanted to be able to leave the shop early some days and go home to cook for Philip. It felt rather awkward being behind the wheel after all those years, but in time it came back to her. Philip let her drive most of the time so she would feel at ease when she took the driving test. They
~~~

thought it would seem odd to his family if she didn't drive and questions might be asked. They were still wary to keep her past a secret.

~28~

"Are you sure you're ready for all of this?" Philip asked Marian as they waited for the bus that would bring his son and family from the airport.

"I think so," she answered, smiling at him. He loved when she smiled, he loved everything about her.

"Here it comes, right on time," Philip said, glancing at his watch. They watched the bus pull into the station and Marian was reminded of the many bus trips she had taken. "That's Katie! See her? She's waving to us," he said excitedly. They got out of the car and walked into the station.

The introductions were done quickly and they made their way to the car. Philip put the luggage into the trunk and off they went. They would stay in the condo with Philip for two days and then a motel. Marian had planned a lunch for them so they could be at home instead of a restaurant, she was eager to get to know them, especially that sweet little girl that she'd heard so much about. Philip proudly showed them around his new home and they were impressed, it was warm and homey.

"Can I call you Grandma then if you live with Grandpa?" Katie asked. Her dad started to say something when Marian interrupted him.

"I think I would like that very much," Marian said, and got down on one knee in front of Katie. The little girl put her arms around Marian's neck and squeezed hard, much like Megan had done all those years ago. A tear came to her eyes and she hugged her back. "Now, let's have some lunch. Is everyone hungry? Uncle Lance is coming over later, Katie. Want to help me with lunch?" Marian was babbling - she couldn't help it, she was so happy. Margaret and Katie helped Marian set out the lunch that she had prepared and the men were talking in the living room.

They were cleaning up after the meal when Lance rang the doorbell. He came in and swooped Katie up in his arms. "How's my best niece? Did ya miss me?" he asked, kissing her. She nodded and squirmed to get down.

"Come see who's here," she said, taking his hand and pointing to Marian. "This is Grandma!"

"Oh, now it's Grandma?" he asked, with a puzzled look.

"Yes, she's Grandma 'cause she's gonna live with Grandpa," Katie told him, matter of factly. They had a wonderful visit and Marian was sad when it was time for her to go. Philip drove her home and went inside with her.

"Only two more days, Marian," he said, holding her close.

"Mrs. Philip Youngberg," she said softly and kissed him. "I'll be very happy not to have to say good-bye and send you home, my love."

"Me too," he told her. "Jenna is working tomorrow all day. I think I'll give her a bonus, what do you think?" He included her in all business decisions now.

"I think we should, she's helped a lot lately," she said. The *we* didn't go unnoticed by Philip, they were indeed a couple now.

The next day was spent together, all of them getting to know one another better. The following day was the wedding - the shop would be closed. A sign on the door read:

Closed this weekend for our wedding. We'll be back on Monday.

It was a rare thing to have a whole weekend off.

~~~

"Philip, do you take this woman . . . ," the minister read from the book in his hand.

" . . . until death do you part?"

"I do," Philip said, in a barely audible voice.

"Marian, do you take this man to be your lawfully wedded husband . . . "

"I do," Marian said loudly.

"The rings please . . . ," and so it went - they became husband and wife. The bride was radiant and she felt as good as she looked. Philip looked handsome in his dark suit and many pictures were taken before they left the chapel; all would be put into an album that Marian would keep for the rest of their lives together. The best part of her life would be recorded in photographs.

They drove to the restaurant together as a married couple. A small room was reserved there for
~~~

the wedding dinner. Marian sat close to Philip in the car.

"Thank you for loving me, Philip," she whispered.

"Well, it isn't hard to do, you know," he said laughing.

"I'm serious. I thought I'd be alone for the rest of my life, but now I have you. I love you," she said, and rested her head on his shoulder. "I really do."

"We made all those promises at the church, but I have one more thing that I want you to promise me," he said seriously.

"What is that?" she asked puzzled.

"I want you to promise me that you'll never make French dip for dinner."

"Oh, Philip! Shame on you . . . you're terrible, do you know that?" she told him and laughed.

"I'm sorry, Marian," he said, pulling her close to him. "I shouldn't have said that and I'm not making light of it. I just couldn't resist." Nothing could daunt his spirits on this special day, not even thoughts of murder, but he hoped he hadn't hurt her.

Never before had she been able to talk about her past in this way. She had never thought of, or talked about the incident, and laughed at the same time. She still regretted what she had done, but maybe now, finally, her conscience was assuaged, thanks to Matthew Tulley and this wonderful man beside her.

~~~

The dinner was delicious, everyone had a won-
~~~

derful time, eating, talking, laughing and just getting to know each other better. Katie insisted on sitting next to her new grandma, which pleased Marian, who was absolutely glowing. The groom was happy too, he never stopped smiling. Phil and Lance were grateful their father had found happiness again, they hadn't seen him like this since their mother was alive. After dessert, coffee and much more conversation, the newly weds said their good-byes and left for the bed and breakfast, and their first night together as man and wife. Phil and his family went back to the condo and were able to talk Lance into spending the night with them there. It was the happiest reunion the family had had in a very long time, and they made the most of it.

~29~

"Mrs. Youngberg!" Philip called to Marian from the back room where he was arranging flowers.

Marian laughed, "Yes, that's me," she said, going to the back of the shop to see what he needed. They had been married one month and still felt like kids in love.

"Since tonight is our one month anniversary, I'm taking care of dinner," he told her. He had a surprise for her and with Jenna's help, he had managed to keep it from Marian.

"Oh, I hope you're not making hotdogs," she said, teasing him. She really wouldn't have cared if he did.

"No, not hotdogs. I want you to go home early and get ready to go out. We're going to that fancy place that we've been wanting to try. Is that all right with you?" he asked.

"Of course - sounds great."

Marian left the shop early as planned. She loved going home, the condo seemed to welcome her each time she entered. It was always sunny, bright, and inviting; and *always* a vase full of yellow tulips sat on the table by the front window. My home, she thought, as she checked the mail and picked out what she would wear for dinner. He said it was fancy, so she chose the nicest dress she had. She was sure Philip would wear a suit. What would he plan for their one year anniversary, she wondered as she showered and washed her hair. Today was only a one month anniversary, but he seemed to have something special planned and had been a bit secretive this past week. She had caught him and Jenna talking quietly together more than once. She had no idea what was going on and didn't give it much thought.

Philip arrived home a little after six, showered, shaved, and they were on their way, both dressed to the nines. The restaurant was indeed fancy and they were happy they had dressed as they did. Beef Wellington was the speciality of the house so they ordered that and shared a bottle of expensive red wine.

"This is very good," Philip whispered to her halfway through the meal, "but I like yours better." She smiled and took a sip of wine. When they finished dessert, Philip excused himself and left the table. Marian assumed he went to the men's room, but he didn't. He called their home to alert Jenna that they would be home in a few minutes.

"Okay. I'll leave now, I think everything will be all right. I'll leave the key under the mat," she told him.

"Thanks for the help, Jenna. She doesn't have a clue, I'm sure," Philip said.

~~~
~~~

When they opened the door to their home, Philip hesitated and looked around the room.

"What's wrong? What are you looking for?" Marian asked him.

"Nothing. Ah, I just didn't remember leaving a light on," he said.

"I always turn it on if we won't be home until dark," she told him, as she hung up her coat in the front closet. Then she heard something in the kitchen. She stopped and listened. "Did you hear that?" she asked.

"What? I didn't hear anything." But he did. A faint cry. "Go see what it is," he told her. She gave him a puzzled look, went into the kitchen and turned on the light, just as a tiny kitten crawled out of a wicker basket.

"Oh, Philip, come here! Where did this . . . Oh, it was you, wasn't it? How did you do this? Isn't it sweet?" she said, picking up the tiny animal and nuzzling its head.

"Do you like her?" he asked. "Jenna helped me, she's been at her house since yesterday."

"I love . . . you said her? It's a girl?" she asked.

He nodded.

"I'm glad it is; I had a girl before. What should we name her?"

"We'll think of something," he told her. "Happy one month anniversary."

"Thank you so much," she said, kissing him. I've wanted a cat for a long time."

"I knew that, so Jenna watched the ads in the paper for me and we picked her out together. I hope you like her," he said.

"I love her and I love you, Philip," she told him and kissed him again.

~~~

The little feline was named Martha, after one week of watching her and getting to know her. The name seemed to fit. Every day Martha went to work with her new family and a small space on the window seat was cleared of tulips so she could nap in the sun. No one passed the shop without stopping to look at the tiny tiger cat curled up sleeping amidst the flowers, and most of them came in and bought tulips, as they were still $4.00 a bunch.

Marian was happier than she had ever been. She loved this man with all her heart and they would work side by side for many years in their little Tulip Hut with Martha. They seldom talked of past things anymore as their new life began when they married and Marian kept up the photo album as planned. Every event in this new life was recorded in pictures. Their family grew to include a new daughter-in-law and three more grandchildren - life was good, and Marian Youngberg no longer had thoughts of regrets.
~~~

About the Author

Fiction writer K. M. Swan started writing when she was in her fifties. After high school she completed nurses training and became a registered nurse. The Rockford author then married, raised four children and worked part-time as a nurse. She now has three grandchildren and enjoys writing about things that are important to her. Her novels are described as inspiring, compelling, heartwarming and easy-to-read stories that bring out the importance of family.

The Novels of
K. M. Swan

If you enjoyed reading *Regrets* and would like additional copies or information about her other novels:

- *The Loft*
- *Catherine's Choice*
- *Sarah*
- *The Journals*

Please mail your request to:

K. M. Swan Books
P.O. Box 8673
Rockford IL 61126

Check your local bookstore for availability.

Or visit our Web site at: www.kmswanbooks.com